TELL 'EM THEY'RE DREAMING

AN ANTHOLOGY

BEDTIME BALLADS & TALL TALES
FROM THE AUSTRALIAN BUSH

Published by Share Your Story
Share Your Story
PO BOX 5447
Alexandra Hills QLD 4161
Printed by Ingram Sparks

First published in Australia 2020
This edition published 2020
Copyright © Michelle Worthington 2020
Cover design, typesetting: WorkingType (www.workingtype.com.au)
Photograph supplied by Photography by Marzena

Worthington, Michelle
Tell em They're Dreamng
ISBN Paperback 9780648773207
ISBN Ebook 9780648773214
pp172

Acknowledgement of Country — we would like to pay respect and acknowledge Aboriginal and Torres Strait Islander peoples as the traditional custodians of the land, rivers and sea. We acknowledge and pay respect to the Elders, past, present and emerging, of all nations.

CONTENTS

PROLOGUE

Forgetting How the Banjo Works

by David Perkins

Oh no! Oh no! How does it go?
That poem I forgot.
It went, 'something something something...'
I've forgot the flamin' lot.

It had bits about some bicycle
That grew a bushy beard
Or was it a bearded cyclist?
It's completely disappeared.

Oh, how's it go? It's an epic verse
But I forgot to bring it.
I should have set it all to music,
I'd recall it if I sing it.

There's a tuckerbox below dog
But that part I forget.
It goes something like 'the dog on top
had come from old regret.'

But some of it I must admit
I've deliberately erased.
It's irrational, illogical
And absolutely crazed!

'And the man from snowy river
let the pony have his head?'
Well, if he gave his head away
How come he isn't dead?

There's bits about a jolly bloke
Who went waltzing with Matilda,
A sheep who rode upon his back,
Apparently, Andy killed her.

I've forgotten all the words in it
And even who it's by.
I think he's from the snowy river,
Five miles from Gundagai.

It probably is for the best
That I forgot this verse.
Instead I'll play banjo now
And that is even worse!

A Very Australian Story

by Elizabeth Macintosh

Let me tell you about old Jack Thomas. He had a racehorse out the back of Woop Woop and it was the light of his life. The nag was called Flying Pieman, but it didn't fly and Jack needed a big win to keep the wolf from the door.

Flying Pieman wasn't much chop as a racehorse. He'd run twenty times for only one win and that was back at his first start ages ago. The only time he'd shown a clean pair of heels was in a field of six. Usually he ran like a hairy goat.

What about his breeding, you ask? Well, he was by The Baker out of Chief Cook. What chance did the horse have?

Jack didn't have a brass razoo. Training racehorses was a dog's life, but Jack believed that every dog has its day and that sooner or later, Flying Pieman would bring home the bacon.

Old Jack decided to go after a quid in the big smoke. He was like a fish out of water, but he had a bee in his bonnet that the Carbine Cup was the race where Flying Pieman would win fame and fortune. Just quietly, I thought Jack was a sandwich short of a picnic and had a few kangaroos loose in the top paddock.

He took the bull by the horns and borrowed money to pay the entry fee. I didn't want him to make a galah of himself, but he was pig-headed about it. Jack had even decided how he'd spend the big bickies that Flying Pieman would win but that was putting the cart before the horse and counting your chickens before they're hatched.

On race day it was raining cats and dogs. Jack assured us he had it straight from the horse's mouth that Flying Pieman was a good thing and that it was chafing at the bit. Jack's confidence started to get on my goat. I admit the horse was toey and in good nick, but it had Buckley's chance.

Between you and me, I wondered how the race committee even allowed Flying Pieman to enter. Maybe Jack slipped someone a few extra quid. Maybe he ear bashed them until the cows came home.

Well, Flying Pieman shot through like a Bondi tram and led all the way. You could have knocked me over with a feather. I wished I'd had a flutter.

Anyway, the stewards were in a tizz and some of the punters were going crook. About the only ones who didn't have a beef were the bookies. I began to smell a rat. Maybe old Jack was a snake in the grass, but I didn't want to make a mountain out of a molehill. If he wanted to feather his own nest, by fair means or foul, I wasn't going to act the goat about it.

I had to admit that I'd been wrong. I'd thought Jack was away with the pixies when he entered Flying Pieman in the Carbine Cup. Thought he was bats, a brick short of a load, but I didn't want to see him go down the gurgler.

Later I asked Jack why he'd been so confident. Stone the crows, the whole thing was off like a bucket of prawns. He told me that Flying Pieman's last nineteen races had been on dry tracks. So what, you ask? Then Jack let the penny slip that the horse was a mud lark and that if it hadn't been wet, he'd planned to take along some locals to perform a rain dance.

I sat there like a stunned mullet. Jack was a crafty old codger all right, although I still wasn't satisfied because Flying Pieman had only ever been the champ once before.

You know what Jack said? In the first race Flying Pieman won, he beat Peter Pan and we all know that it won the Melbourne Cup twice!

I retired, defeated. There never were any kangaroos loose in the top paddock after all.

Abigail's Tale

by Mark and Suan Wuschke

'Ah-choo! Ahh-choooo! Ahhh-chooooooo!' Woken again! It's the lady who lives up on the hill behind our sleeping tree. She sneezes three times every morning. We call her the sneeze lady. Brrrrr! I hate waking up early in winter!

'Abigail, breakfast!' our mother sings. So much for sleeping! I wonder what we'll find today. 'Beatrice! Charlie! Let's go!' They fly up to the branch where Mum is already perched. My brother is always eager to get up. But Beatrice takes forever, always pruning her feathers so they look just right.

We take off on our breakfast tour, flying over the brown fields, dry creeks and dams. Mum looks for farmhouses. Our favorite family, in the house with the creaky windmill, has set out little bits of meat for us!

Mother lands first and casts a sharp eye around for danger. We fly down to the feeder and have our fill.

We're thirsty! We fly to Pullen Creek, where there's always a few pools, even when it hasn't rained for a long time. 'Remember little chicks, drink one at a time. Two of you keep watch!' says our Mum.

'We know Mum!' Beatrice says.

'I know you know,' says Mum, 'but be careful. I saw a fox drinking there yesterday.'

But today there's nothing dangerous, and we have a good drink. Two cranky magpies fly over. 'Push aside, Curra-*wrongs!*' says the biggest magpie, who likes to tease us. 'Go home, *rag*-pies!' says Charlie.

We fly back to our sleeping tree, a big old iron bark. After playing for a while, I feel my eyes getting heavy.

It's nearly sunset when I wake. 'Get up, lazy bones, dinner time! We're waiting for you!' says my little sister. On our dinner trip, we find a tray of sunflower seeds that a family set out for us. Our favorite! We crack them open, one by one. Yummy!

'Enough you lot! Bed time!' says Mum. She takes to the air, and we follow close behind, since it's getting dark and we don't want to get lost. Back on my branch in our sleeping tree, I tuck my head under my wing. 'Goodnight

Abigail!' sings mum. 'Goodnight, mother,' I whisper, and fall asleep.

'Ah-choo! Ahh-choooo! Ahhh-choooooo!'

'Breakfast, children!' But today I don't want to wake up. I'll sleep for five more minutes. But it's an hour when I wake again. I look around for mother, but she's not here. 'Mother? Beatrice? Charlie?' I sing. 'Curra-wong, CURRA-WONG!' I call as loud as I can. But they don't hear.

I'll have to get my own breakfast. I fly to the house with the windmill. But their feeder is empty, not one scrap left!

I fly to other houses that sometimes set out food. There is some seed at one, but a flock of cockatoos is there, and they won't let me land. I'll have to find food in the fields. Mother taught us to find tasty beetles, skinks or grubs, but I'm no good at finding them. I sit on a rock, looking and listening carefully for anything moving in the dry grass. There! A beetle! I swoop to get it, but it has crawled away into its burrow. I dig a little, but it's gone. Grrrr! I return to my perch, and wait, but there's nothing to eat.

I'm thirsty! I fly over to the creek, and land at the water's edge. I feel uneasy, drinking alone. I lean forward for another sip. Something is rushing up behind me! A goanna! I leap in the air, as it lunges. It catches my tail feathers! I flap as hard as I can; the feathers come off in his mouth, but I get away! Without my tail feathers, it's so hard to fly, and I soon tumble to the ground. I look back; the goanna has spit out the feathers and is coming at me!

I fly, and run, this way and that. Past trees and fields and fences. On and on, not knowing where I am going. Finally, I fall exhausted to the ground. It is nearly dark. I am too weak to fly up into a tree for the night. Frightened, I hide and sleep the best I can.

'Who's in my veggie patch!' says a loud voice. A woman with a pink scarf towers over me. I want to fly, but my wings are too stiff. 'Are you hurt?' she asks. I try to hop away, but my legs are stiff too. 'You have no tail feathers! It's a good thing I found you, before Normie did.' She picks me up. 'Curra-wong!' I whisper. *Please don't eat me!* But she doesn't hurt me; she brings me inside her house and puts me in a box with a soft towel for a bed. She sets down a tray of seeds with bits of meat. 'You must be hungry, little currawong. Eat all you want, I'll leave you in peace.' It doesn't seem she'll hurt me. I'm so hungry! I peck away until I've emptied the dish. Tired and full, I sleep.

She peeks in the next day. 'You are going to be

fine. Those feathers will grow back in a week or two. Try not to move too much, for your own safety.' She carries my box out to the veranda and sets it high on a shelf. 'You'll be safe from Normie up here.' I wonder, who is Normie?

A few days go by. My tail feathers start to grow back, and my aching wings and legs heal. The lady comes to visit twice a day, bringing me food and water.

At last I am strong enough to fly up to the edge of the box. I have a good view of the garden. In the middle is a big jacaranda tree with pretty purple flowers. She is growing vegetables, too, I see rows of cabbages. I am almost well enough to fly home now – but where is home? Getting lost scares me; I hop back down to my bed.

Day after day, my feathers grow. Late one afternoon, I jump up to have a look around. I test my wings, and they are strong enough to fly. How I miss my mum! And my brother and sister. Tears come to my eyes. I want to go home! I miss our sleeping tree, and the sneeze lady. 'Curra-wong!' I sing sadly. Where are you all?

But somebody heard me. Below on the veranda, a cat is creeping towards me, with his hungry eyes on me! I'm sure this box is out of his reach. Or is it? He creeps closer. If I fly now, could I fly far enough to escape him? I flap my wings as hard as I can. The cat leaps in the air! I fly just in time, as the box goes crashing to the floor.

'Normie!' cries the woman, who rushes out of the house. I manage to fly to the clothes line. But the cat is still following me. 'Fly little one, fly!' shouts the lady, and I take to the air, flying as hard as I can. I made it! I fly high up into the branches of the Jacaranda. I am safe here! I rest for a moment. The cat looks up at me, sulking. You'll not eat me today, Normie.

I take off and fly higher. I am looking for something familiar, but I can't see any place I know. I am lost! I continue flying over the brown fields, the dry dams. It is getting dark, and I'll have to spend the night alone. I cry a little, as I tuck my head into my wing.

'Ah-choo!' Did I hear something? Or was I dreaming?

'Ahh-choooo!' There it is again!

'Ahhh-choooooo!' It's the sneeze lady! Though it's far away, I know it's her! I spring up and fly towards the sound. There's the house with the windmill! There's our sleeping tree! I fly to the top, where Beatrice and Charlie are still asleep.

'Breakfast!' I sing to them. 'Up you get!'

'What! Is that you Abigail! Mum, come quick, it's

13

Abigail!' Mum flies over too and embraces me with her big wings. 'Abbie! You're back!'

I tell them the whole story of my tail feathers and the lady with the pink scarf.

'What house was she in?' asks mum.

'The one with a jacaranda in the garden.'

'Did it have a cabbage patch?'

'Yes.'

'I know that house! There's a cat living there!' I tell her he *nearly* got me.

Anyway, I never sleep in anymore. When the sneeze lady wakes us, I'm the first one up. Some days we all fly over to the lady's house, and perch in her Jacaranda tree. 'Currawong, currawong!' we sing to her, thanking her for saving me.

She comes to the window and waves. 'Good morning little Currawongs! Be careful of Normie!'

Australia's Largest Talent

by Trish Donald

It was a glorious day, a perfect day for the big competition. Every year Cicada looked forward to it but this year was special, this year he was old enough to compete. The conditions were perfect, he was sure the cicada family would win. There was great excitement on the trunk of the old eucalyptus where he, his family and all his cousins lived. Everyone was flicking their wings and stretching their ribs practicing and warming up.

A stage of giant granite boulders in the centre of a clearing had been thoroughly swept for the occasion. The judging panel of expert listeners — two Owls, and a Tawny Frogmouth — who were usually asleep at this time of the day — sat alert in front of the stage ready for the first contestants. A large crowd had gathered behind the judges, there was a great chattering in anticipation and excitement.

The first contestants on stage were an Emu family. They fluffed their feathers and the dad started grunting. He was soon joined by the mother's loud booming while their five chicks began to whistle. The crowd cheered and clapped. It was a fabulous performance and the judges scribbled notes earnestly on their official note pads.

Next came the Magpies who swooped in from the skies gracefully. They chortled and carolled, mesmerizing everyone with their fluty melodies. There was much nodding and agreement in the crowd, they sounded beautiful, but they weren't very loud and Cicada knew they would be easy to beat!

Then came the Cockatoos. They screamed and shrieked until the judges raised their wings indicating their time was up, but they were so busy shrieking they didn't notice. Eventually the Kookaburras shooed them off with their alarm clock chuckles! It was such a funny site to see the Kookaburras chasing away the attention hungry Cockatoos that soon everyone in the crowd was laughing uproariously. The Cockatoos screeched back in protest, but the judges did not flinch. Cicada was worried, how could they ever beat them? He looked at the judges, but they gave nothing away.

A group of Stick Insects who were led onto the stage by a friendly Koala were next. They sat very still soon disappearing due to their camouflage. The crowd though confused, waited patiently and gave them a clap for their effort. Unfortunately, the clapping startled the Stick Insects who reappeared in a leap of fright which brought Koala rushing to their rescue. Everyone wondered if they had fallen asleep, but nobody said anything. The rules of the competition meant everyone was allowed to compete. Cicada breathed a sigh of relief; he knew they would definitely beat the Stick Insects.

The competition continued and the sun was getting high in the sky. There were a few more groups to go until it was Cicadas turn, they would be the last group to perform. An ancient Cassowary with a deep low rumble booming from its chest took centre stage. The sound permeated the bush around them and lasted for several minutes. Cicada was impressed that one animal could make such a deep sound. Everyone clapped, especially Cicada.

To everyone's surprise a scourge of Mosquito was next but nobody could hear them until they swarmed off the stage into the crowd. Circling closer and closer towards everyone's ears, their high pitch whining became piercing, unpleasant and annoying. The judges lent in, talking in hushed tones then held up red cards. The Mosquitoes were disqualified because they had left the stage. Everyone was relieved when the winging Mosquitoes left, a few animals had started scratching.

There was one more act then it would be time for Cicadas big debut. Cicada was getting very nervous, but he tried to calm himself by focusing on the next competitors, the Lyrebirds. Cicada's heart sank, he knew Lyrebirds were particularly skilled with sounds. He had heard them in the bush mimicking other animals. And that is just what they did. They impersonated the Emu family, the chortling Magpies, the screaming Cockatoos, and the belly laughing Kookaburras. They did not imitate the Stick Insects because there was no sound to mimic but they did an impressive impersonation of the Cassowary. To be kind to everyone's ears they decided not to impersonate the Mosquitos.

On and on they went, imitating with such accuracy that it was hard to tell the difference between the Lyrebird and the original maker of the sounds. They even threw in some twanging and clacking for good measure. The crowd was mesmerised, the judges seem transfixed too. But Cicada realized there was one sound that they did not mimic. To Cicadas surprise, one sound was missing. Hope rose in Cicada.

When the Lyrebirds finished, the crowd sat in stunned silence, a mixture of awe and wonder on their faces. The sun had risen above everyone's heads. The sky was hazy from the heat. The competition was almost at an end. On flew Cicada and his family, the last act. Cicada was so nervous he could barely contain himself. He looked around at his family, at his parents and his cousins, all smiling, all happy that Cicada was now old enough to join them. And then they began.

As one, they flexed their muscles, bending, curving, kinking and contracting. Louder and louder they got. Cicada could feel himself drawn in until they sang as one. Louder and louder until a crescendo of sound rang through the bush. It was beautiful, it was piercing, and it was LOUD! Cicada looked out to the audience, everyone was covering their ears, including the judges, and he swelled with pride, they had done it, they had beaten all the other animals. They were the loudest. They had won the title of Australia's LOUDEST Talent! The sound of the cicadas was replaced by the thunderous clapping from the crowd. There was a standing ovation as the Judges handed over the winning trophy.

That night, as Cicada went to sleep, he looked up at the old Eucalyptus to where the trophy had been placed. What a day it had been, what a thrill, his first competition and they had won. He drifted off to sleep with the sound of his family ringing through the bush in celebration.

Banjo

by Michelle Worthington

'Twas half a mile from Corryong,
In a tumble jumble shack,
There lived a little hobo
Who went by the name of Jack.

He dressed himself in battered clothes,
Was hardly ever seen,
And worked as hard as older men,
Was just as tough and lean.

He took a job at Greg Greg
To run cattle up the Tom,
He never told and no one asked,
Just where he had come from.

There never was, and never still,
From Black Rock to the sea,
Drover, stock or master,
There was none could ride like he.

As riding was his special gift,
And true his only one,
It captured the attention
Of a farming Scotsman's son.

There was something unassuming
That kept to tweak his mind.
Andrew would take to follow him,
To see what he may find.

For there he'd wait, while cattle moved
Along the Khancoban:
For a glimpse of Jack who'd grow into
A Snowy River Man.

Back when a growing nation,
Which sought to make a mark,
Did grow a burning ember
Into a brilliant spark.

Jack was quick with whip and spur
And Andrew, as a boy,
Could make the simple written work
An uncommon piece of joy.

It struck him then, young as he was,
That something could be done
To reach both town and country,
To unite them both as one.

So, he began to write an ode
To those like his friend Jack,
About how one man dared and won
To get his courage back.

'Twas young Andrew, from Narambla,
That made a legend strong.
The stirring power of his words
Forever will live on.

When a country short of heroes
Was looking for the bold,
A man they would call Banjo
Shined his light with stories told

Around low burning fires,
And schools in every town,
How we can always rise above
When others put us down.

Today we hear the calling,
'When everyone is free,
With courage, hope and action,
We'll be all that we can be.'

'

Burn Lantana, Burn

by Kayt Duncan

Dazza built a bonza shed
 out near Boonaroo.
He really did a bang-up job,
 all his angles true.

When haulin' in his brewin' gear he
 popped his disc; L3.
Fallin' down upon the ground cried,
 'Missus! Please help me!'

Burn Lantana, burn. Burn, Lantana burn.
Posies of colour, denying all others,
to take up some turf in their turn.
So burn Lantana, burn.

Umpteen months the shed just stood,
    unloved yet still pristine.
Below the surface, alive with purpose,
    Lantana roots, unseen.

Dazza'd kept that beast at bay,
    now poison went unspent.
Christmas came Lantana's way
    and up the walls, it went.

Latching to the window sills, and
    clinging to the eaves,
Lantana claimed 'Man's Cave' that day,
    with flowers, thorns, and leaves.

Burn Lantana, burn. Burn, Lantana burn.
Posies of colour, denying all others,
to take up some turf in their turn.
So burn Lantana, burn.

Wheelchair-bound our Dazza found,
    tears that fell anew.
His shed was lost behind thick thorns, and
    now his mood was too.

His Missus took a trip to Bunnings, and
　　got herself a blade.
She slashed and slashed at long thin stems,
　　but little dent was made.

　　Burn Lantana, burn. Burn, Lantana burn.
　　Posies of colour, denying all others,
　　to take up some turf in their turn.
　　So burn Lantana, burn.

The 'black dog' sat with Dazza daily, so
　　Missus up'd the game.
She siphoned petrol from the ute;
　　accelerant for flame.

She took a match. She lit it up.
　　The fire was alive.
Flames danced and dined on wooden vine,
　　No chance it would survive.

Come the dawn the weed was gone, alas
　　the shed was too.
But Dazza grinned. He'd build again, and
　　Bluescope Steel'd do.

Burn Lantana, burn. Burn, Lantana burn.
Posies of colour, denying all others,
to take up some turf in their turn.
So burn Lantana, burn.

Bush Ballad

by M. J. Gibbs

It's time to tell a bush tale,
Of creatures wild and free
Of Aussie male and female,
That meet beneath a tree.

The kangaroos come bounding in
The python slithers and slides.
The kookaburras cackle with a din,
Opossum gracefully glides.

From bracken swamp comes salty Croc
His billabong mates slide too,
Ahead is brown striped frog — tick tock
And wombat eating his stew.

Each of the animals find their way
Beneath the old gum tree,
To hear and have their personal say
A rich diversity.

Brush turkey bickers at the verse
A ballad for the night,
The rumble grows a little worse
The animals begin to fight.

Dingo howls, kangaroo thumps
Sugar glider breaks free;
Sand goanna sprints and jumps
At spiky devil up the tree.

'Sit down, bush creatures, don't take flight,'
It's about a sunburnt country.
A poem that brings us pure delight
Wide brown lands for you and me.

Lorikeet and dingo dog
Listen to the rhyme,
Kangaroo plays the digeridoo
While others tap in time.

'I love her far horizons,
I love her jewel-sea,'
Her beauty, hiss the snakes,
In slithering harmony.

'I'm much too busy,' says bandicoot
His long nose quite absurd
Magpie declares, 'it's rather cute
To hear the power of words.'

The moon mirrors on rippled sands,
The animals fall asleep
Snuggled up beneath a tree
Shut eyes and do not peep.

Good night bush creatures, young and old,
The speckled stars play tune;
The heavens shine a brilliant gold
It will be morning soon.

Campfire Crackles, Ripstiks Curl

by Maria Parenti

Campfire crackles.
Camp oven simmers.
Coals pulse, embers glow.

Hearty bushman stew.
Rump steak, scrubbed potatoes,
chopped celery, sliced carrots, diced onions,
all basting in a storm of flavours.
Two pinchful grated ginger and
one secret ingredient to sweeten.

Mmm...
campfire, savoury stew

wafting, weaving

up to the timber verandah...

... to three kids playing on Ripstiks.

Slimline mini skateboards

bottoms neatly fit into its scooped deck.

Legs out straight,

hands steer onto floor.

Ripstiks wind round

verandah obstacle course,

on pivoting 360 casters.

A cry goes up.

Let's race.

First one gets beef stew!

Take... your... positions.

3... 2...

'Come and set the table,' calls Mum.

...1. Go!

One Ripstik swerves right at lounge.
Three riders race down straight,
past outdoor dining table.
One rider must take corner first.
Hands roll.
Pull, roll. Pull.
Ripstiks speed forward.
Floor boards grumble.
Right hand, left hand,
pull.

Corner of table coming up fast.
No-one's backing off!
Youngest rider lifts hand.
Two oldest power on
shoulder to shoulder.
One has to back off soon.
No one breathes.
Only one can take corner first.
'Back off!' yells youngest.

'At least bring down the spoons,' Mum calls.

Lean in right.

Turn, turn, turn.

Both riders turn in parallel.

Outside rider works harder.

Big pull right hand.

Lean right, slight nudge!

Ooh!

Inside rider loses tenth of a second.

Outside riders leads straight-on.

'You did that on purpose!' yells inside rider.

'Yeh, well, you were, too... .'

'Bring down the glasses,' calls Mum.

'Come on!' yells youngest.

All three scramble back on Ripstiks.

'Prepare for the chase!'

'I'm being chased by the police.'

'You're going the wrong way.'

Winning rider speeds off yelling,

'Good bye moo-cha-cha!'

Youngest falls off Ripstik.
Now she's on foot, chasing other two.
'Red light, red light.'
I said, 'Red Light!'
'What does that mean?'
'It means stop!'
But no one stops.

'Bring down the soup bowls,' calls Mum.

'Did you see that? I delayed the officer.'
'Reverse, reverse, reverse!'
Two Ripstiks slide sideways.
Two run stick-less.
'Don't try and trip me.'
'Halt!'
'What you doing?'

'Back on sticks,' yells youngest.
Swerving, turning, near missing.

Crasshh!
Collision of legs, arms, Ripstiks tangle.

Dad yells, 'Grubs on! First one down gets double beef stew.'

'I'm first,' yells youngest.
'No, I'm first.'
'No, I am.'

Push. Shove. Legs, arms untangle. Ripstiks flung to side.

Three kids line up, bowls in one hand,
warm damper in the other.

Dad scowls,
Mum taps foot.

Youngest glides forward.
Thick beef stew ladled.
Mmm...
as campfire crackles.

Dave in the Wild West

by Paula Stevenson

At our farm we have a guy called Dave. He can fix anything. He can mend machinery and build gates and fences out of bits of piping. He can pour concrete, fix plaster board and repair leaky gutters. He can muster, mark calves and wrestle escaped weaners who leap out of the calf crush. Sometimes our farm is like the Wild West!

He is also handy with equipment. Dad has a quad bike that has been a load of trouble and spends more time at the garage than on the farm. It always breaks down when we need it most, like when we are mustering

One day, Dave was helping us muster but the bike only lasted half an hour as it was overheating and had to be abandoned. That afternoon, Dave let me watch. 'Watch and learn,' he said. I squatted on a bit of cardboard beside him in the shed.

He stripped the front off, found some loose wires that were shorting, sorted those out, and then discovered that the radiator was not even on its mountings. He reattached the front grille with some left-over buttons from the calf marking. They made very handy clips.

Dave also helps out by spraying our paddocks. But one day he became impatient waiting for us to bring down some stakes so he could mark where he had been. He took off his shirt. Mum had noticed it the day before; seemed to be a nice item, soft material and a checked pattern...a bit different from the orange High Vis shirts Dave usually wears.

By the time we arrived, Dave had started on the markers, by ripping up the sleeves of his shirt. When he showed us what was left, Mum noticed the label inside the collar... a very posh brand. When she told Dave, he was unimpressed.

Dave loves our wildlife. We have roos, wallabies, wombats, deer, rabbits and hares and snakes... everywhere. Today Dave killed the huge brown snake that I had nearly trodden on in the backyard. They are dangerous and I would not like to be bitten and rushed off to hospital. But maybe a helicopter ride would be fun!

Dave had been napping on the back of a wooden

trailer after lunch. When he woke, he swung his legs over the side, looked down and between his feet was the brown snake. He pulled his feet back up very quickly, then reached for a short piece of black poly pipe. He whacked it across the neck. He even took it away at the end of the day and put it down a gully so the dogs would not be tempted to take a bite and be affected by the poison.

Mustering and fencing provide opportunities for Dave to catch some wildlife. Coming back from a far paddock, I saw Dave suddenly leap off his bike and run into the long grass. He scooped up something and stuffed it down his jumper. What was it? Some ducks? Or a goanna?

'What's that wriggling in there?' I asked.

'Some fat little wild pigs,' he said. 'Going to take 'em home and fatten 'em.'

He locked them in the back of his ute in a box until it was time to go home.

One morning Dave arrived and said, 'Have a geek in my toolbox.'

I lifted the lid of the toolbox and there was a wedge tailed eagle!

I hoped it wasn't dead.

Dave had found it on the side of the road. None of us

were sure what injuries it had, but just a short time later, it flapped out of the toolbox and leapt from the back of the ute. Didn't seem to be able to fly though.

Mum got the number for Wires and we told them about it.

Dave scooped it up and secured it back into his ute in case the dogs thought they might play with it.

The Wires people came and put it in a cage, took note of where it had been found and said they would let us know.

The good part of this story is the ending!

They rang a few weeks later and asked if we wanted to come down and see the eagle released.

We all bumped down the road in the ute and watched while the cage door was opened. The huge eagle flapped a bit, staggered down the road, then took off into the sky, heading for the top of a large tree nearby.

It felt so good. Back where he belongs.

And when we drive down that part of the road, if we glance up sometimes, we can see him, surveying the land, on the lookout for a silly rabbit for a feast. I am glad he is back home in the land he loves.

It's a great life, here in the Wild West! For everyone.

I am Listening Bush Bird

by Kim Pullon

Sulphur crested cockatoo bird,
Narrate the tales you see.
Your raucous calls by all are heard!
Outback stories for me?

Through the ochre plains roos bound,
Headed for new-growth green.
For the northern rain has reached this ground,
Your song paints me this scene.

Air is crisp before thermals rise,
And wedgetail wakes to rule.
He takes to sky; I hear your cries -
Fair warning for his fuel.

'Lizards still race in Eulo town,'
So, my cockie will say.
All gathering for race renown,
And trophy on this day.

Frilly neck wins this year again.
Bearded dragon delayed
To talk with thorny devil plain
About his drying glade.

He has not seen the dryness end,
His heart grows filled with fear.
But messages of hope my cockie sends,
'The wet is coming near.'

Sulphur crested cockatoo bird,
Narrate the tales you see.
Your raucous calls by all are heard!
Please, more stories for me?

A carpet python stays entwined
Enjoying sunny rock,
Whilst up above koalas dine,
watching the land's livestock.

You tell me how you play your part,
Commentating the breeze,
While Jacob's cross spiders build art -
Galleries amongst the leaves.

As dunnarts clamber sand ladders
To reach the termites high,
Kookaburras play snakes n' adders
To pass the arvo by.

You tell me of their family creed;
Their cackling 'Gooday!' cry,
Which all brothers and sisters heed.
'We're here!' they unify.

Sulphur crested cockatoo bird,
Narrate the tales you see.
Your raucous calls by all are heard!
Please, more stories for me?

Homemade rainbows — lorikeets add
To quieter scenes they find;
Their romping cheek and hopping mad -
Distractions for our kind.

Long-necked turtles synchronise swim,
While egrets flawless dive.
Banjo frog awards medals at whim;
Billabong games he contrived.

Yabbies compete in Windorah,
Whilst galahs cheer them on.
Magpies swoop in from not so far,
As does the old black swan.

Cockie says Swan's seen the world
But retired where he loved,
Where sun sets red amongst clouds curled,
Before stars travel 'bove.

Gather your mates. Wings, outstretched arms.
Raising crests, rocking heads.
Through sharing your colourful yarns,
You leave nothing unsaid.

Sulphur crested cockatoo bird,
Find your eucalypt bed.
Your stories from today were heard,
Time to rest now overhead.

It's Hot Outside

by Louise Pocock

It's hot outside, my cheeks are pink,
My nose is hiding under zinc.

It's hot outside, a whirring sound,
The ceiling fan goes round and round.

It's hot outside, our legs are sticky.
Pressed on vinyl, feeling iiiicky!

It's hot outside, my ice block drips
All over scattered melon pips.

Outside we find a patch of shade
Where clover blooms and games are played.

Dad turns on the garden hose,
He smiles at me and yells 'here goes!'

A water fight! Balloons in flight!
A stream of water from a height.

They know that I am not a joker
When I get my super soaker!

Mum fills up the paddling pool:
No better way to keep us cool.

We run and jump and splash and sit,
Until the tube begins to split!

Tumbling out, on the ground,
Glistening grass, a muddy mound.

We even have a water slide –
Jump on quick before it dries!

It's hot outside, a game of cricket.
Bowl... HOWZAT?! I took a wicket!

It's hot outside, cicada song.
An insect choir, thousands strong.

It's hot outside, I feel a breeze –
A coolness coming through the trees.

A summer's day, sweet memories.
The best of times on days like these.

It Happened One Day

by Polly Rose

It happened one day about a quarter to four
I was having a nap. I heard a knock at the door.
I groaned a bit. I just wanted to rest.
Peace and quiet is what I like best.

I scrambled up and opened the door.
I blinked in shock at what I saw.
On my step sat a kangaroo.
'Evening,' he said. 'How are you?'

'Pardon,' he added, so polite.
'I wonder if I could stay the night?'
'Stay the night?' I said. 'Sleep in here?
There's just not enough room I fear.'

But the kangaroo bounded right ahead.
When I turned, he was in my bed.
I moved him over and lay there too.
I really didn't know what to do.

We both settled down to have our nap,
When once again I heard a tap.
A wombat sat at my door.
'I promise I almost never snore.'

He lumbered in and joined the roo.
They lay on my bed. What could I do?
I closed my eyes and settled to rest.
At least I tried my very best.

Next night they were back but behind the roo
Was an emu, a koala and a potoroo.
They all curled up on my bed.
I found myself on the floor instead!

They left as soon as it was light
But I knew they'd be back the very next night.
So, when they gathered at my door,
This time I was ready, not like before.

'Listen fellas, this has to cease.
This house is mine. Leave here please.
All I want is peace and quiet
And what I've got is close to a riot.'

They looked very sad; heads hung low.
All was silent as they turned to go.
I watched them heading out the door.
At last! Peace and quiet as before!

I lay to ease my aching head,
But strange I couldn't rest. Instead,
It felt sort of lonely on my own.
I missed my guests. I was all alone.

I thought maybe I'd ask them back.
I went walking up the old bush track.
In a little while, I found the roo,
The wombat, koala and the potoroo!

I said, 'Fellas, come on back.
I know it's only a simple shack
But I miss you animals. It's true.'
The kangaroo said, 'We miss you too.'

So, we chatted together, came up with a plan.
Now whenever I'm lonely or need a hand,
I wander out and visit my friends
Who live in the bush where the garden ends.

It works both ways and they visit here too
And there's something I want to share with you.
If you're ready to go halfway with friends,
It really works out in the end.

It happened one day about a quarter to four.
I was having a nap. I heard a knock at the door.
I smiled and stretched. I knew who it'd be.
You know peace and quiet doesn't suit me!

Larrikin Lyle

by Jill Smith

In 1942, my dad was just a boy. This is based on stories he told me about his growing up.

It was just getting light when I threw my 'Boys Own' almanac comic book off the bed onto the floor. I love Roy Rogers. I'd love to be a cowboy and swing a lasso and ride a horse just like him. I pulled on my old t-shirt and shorts and headed out through the kitchen.

'Don't get into mischief, Lyle. Eat something before you go out.'

'Aw, Mum, it's Saturday and I'm meeting Davo at Black Hill.'

'Have this first!' Mum slid a bowl of porridge across the table as she nodded at the chair. I sat down and began slurping the thick gruel down.

'Don't go getting your bike wheel caught in the tram track like you did last week.'

'Mum, I won't.'

'Off you go then,' she picked up the bowl off the old wooden table. 'Don't go getting filthy dirty.'

'Sure,' I called back as I ran through the back door to the woodshed. I grabbed a hessian bag and my bike and skidded down the drive. We live in Queen Street, Ballarat East and I scooted down the road towards Eureka Stockade, seeing the blue and white southern cross flag flap in the wind. It was cold as I turned towards Black Hill. I cut off before the double wide main street, Sturt Street. It was made in the old mining days by huge bullock drays. My grandpa told me about teams of up to fourteen bullocks pulling a wagon on dirt roads, carving out that main street as they drove up then turned and came back.

I could see Davo waiting.

'Hi, Blue!' he called as he waved madly.

'Spotted your red head from miles away,' he said as Davo shoved me.

'Got your sack?'

'Sure,' he held up a well-worn bag.

'Mum told me not to get grubby,' I said, shaking my head.

'Not much chance of that,' Davo grinned.

'Nope.' I rested my bike beside the big gum near the top. Black Hill was a great muddy slope after the rain. 'Let's go!' I threw myself on my hessian bag and slipped down the grassy muddy slope. With Davo at my side we whooped with joy as we gained speed then skidded to a halt at the bottom.

'Again!' Davo nudged my shoulder and we ran full pelt back up the hill.

A few more times and we were covered in mud.

'That was great, but I reckon we should wash off a bit. Me mum will kill me if she sees me like this.'

'I reckon,' Davo nodded. We collected our bikes. 'Your mum knows you'll get home a wreck. Come to my place and clean up.'

'Yeah. I want to go to the shop and buy some peppermints. Old Maude won't take kindly to mud on her lino shop floor. I've got two-bob from my dad for choppin' wood, to spend.'

'Come on then,' Davo raced ahead and I followed. His place was just around the corner in Eureka Street.

When we skidded up his drive, I pushed Davo over. We laughed. We washed up and dusted off as much mud as we could. We headed out again on our bikes to ride to the lake past the old post office on the corner in Sturt Street, just past the lake.

We took the three stone steps up to the weatherboard building on the corner. It was small and dark inside but for the window and the dim glow of a lamp at the rear of the shop that cast a light over an exciting array of jars on the shelf.

Old Maude came out from the back room to serve us.

'You two look a sight, David Cunningham. And you, Larrikin Lyle, look like something the cat dragged in. What are you wanting?'

'I've got two-bob for sweets, but apart from a couple of all-day suckers, can I get peppermints?' I slid my shiny silver piece onto the counter.

Maude didn't reply. She opened a brown paper bag and started filling it. 'You want the suckers now?'

'Yep,' I nodded and handed one to Davo who gladly popped the sticky ball in his mouth.

'Strawberry! Yum.' I tucked my gob stopper in my cheek and mumbled thanks to the old lady as I took hold of the mint filled bag.

Giggling and laughing like galahs we hopped back on our bikes and headed off around the lake and past the gardens where the begonias were on display, then onto the assortment of cages beyond a gate, the town's zoo.

'The monkeys are that way,' I pointed. We got off the bikes and wheeled them along between us before leaving them against the large cage filled with small, gangly apes.

'We haven't been here for a while. This'll be a hoot!' Dave grinned.

I looked around to see if Albert, the zookeeper, was around.

'It's safe. Here we go. I'll put some in line along the fence.' The chimps sat watching us as I lined up the mints, then they started to get interested.

'The big one's coming over,' Davo giggled.

The large black chimpanzee approached and grabbed a couple of mints, shoving them in his mouth. A couple of other monkeys followed suit. Their reactions to the searing heat in their mouths was to dive down to the water barrel and drink. The peppermint flavour intensified, and the apes started swinging around, puffing out their cheeks and squealing.

We both roared laughing.

'Jeeze, Lyle, that's so funny.'

'Yep,' I grinned.

We started messing around like we were chimps, tickling our underarms and hooting.

'Davo, he's spraying me!'

'Yuck, it stinks! That big chimp is still letting fly and getting me too!' Davo held his nose and backed away.

'Aw, yuck! That's his poo!' I wailed. The chimps were raising a real ruckus and throwing whatever they could at us.

'You're copping it all over. He's got good aim,' Davo ducked as the ape lobbed another well-aimed blob of brown muck.

'Oh no! He's throwing more poo!' I wailed.

Suddenly, Davo grabbed my arm, and pointed down the path.

'Cripes! It's Albert!'

We raced away in the other direction as fast as we could.

'You boys!' Albert roared. 'I'll get you, and you'll clean every cage out for the next month when I do.'

We ran till our sides ached. Puffing, we reached the gate with Albert on our tails.

We jumped on our bikes and raced away, full pelt. We split up and headed to our separate homes. I stank.

'Goodness, Lyle! Get those disgusting clothes off and

go and have a bath. Now!' Mum looked like she'd skin me alive, so I didn't argue.

'To think I told Old Maude you were a good boy.'

'Aw Mum, we didn't do much. We just gave some peppermints to the monkeys at the zoo.'

Mum did her best not to laugh out loud. I could tell she wasn't mad at me.

'You're one Larrikin, Lyle,' Mum said. She was patting tears from her eyes. 'Such a Larrikin, I think I must have been dreaming, to think you could be a good boy.'

Little One

by Christine Crawford

My brother always gets the good jobs. Just because he's four years older than me, he is allowed to ride the little motorbike and go in the truck with Dad to check the fences. He likes anything with motors or wheels; he doesn't really care about the cattle. I like the cattle; they talk to me with their big brown eyes. But as I am only seven, my job is to feed the chickens and collect their eggs.

Davie and I were having breakfast. For once, he hadn't gone out with Dad to check the cows. It would have been before daylight when Dad left and Davie is scared of the dark. I know that because we share a bedroom. We were just finishing our toast when the sound of Dad's ute pulling up reached us. We heard him kick off his boots and clomp inside in his socks.

'Hi boys,' he said. He turned to Davie. 'I've got a job for you. One of the cows is ignoring her calf. I think he's going to need hand rearing. You can do it before and after school.'

I watched as Davie sighed and slumped his shoulders. 'Do I have to, Dad? I've got heaps of schoolwork to do, haven't I Mum?'

I crossed my fingers. Mum always thinks of me. 'What about Sammy?' she said. 'He doesn't have as much homework. He could do it.'

I jumped up. 'Yes, Dad! Yes! Let me do it. Please?' Sometimes Dad looks at me as if he has never seen me before.

'Sammy? Yeah ... I suppose he could manage. '

'Course I could, Dad. Let me, please.'

Dad took the piece of toast Mum handed him. 'Okay, the calf's out the back in the house paddock. Go and have a look.'

I didn't wait to put my boots on properly. One foot went in okay, the other only half way in and I wiggled it on as I hobbled across the yard. A white bundle lay huddled just beyond the wire fence. When I said hello, the calf lifted his head slowly and looked at me with his brown eyes. In that moment I knew we would be best friends. Then there was a rush of hooves and a second calf galloped up. It was bigger and livelier than my calf. The first calf had already become *my* calf.

'You must be hungry,' I said to the two of them. 'Hang on, I'll be back soon.' I raced back inside, shouting, 'Dad, Mum, there are two calves there.'

When I came back into the kitchen only Mum and Dad were there. Davie must have gone to his room, probably to play a game on his iPad. I'm sure I heard Dad say something about '... in a dream world...' I knew they had been talking about me and the calves. 'Sammy,' Mum said, 'don't get too attached to the weaker calf, okay?'

'Your mother's right. That little one won't survive. Don't even bother with it.'

I was shocked. This was my calf. We were best friends. I was most definitely going to feed him. I was too angry to think of anything to say so I stormed out of the kitchen. I went straight to the laundry where all the calf feeding stuff was kept. From a cupboard I took out the big plastic bottles, the long rubber teats and the bag of dried milk powder. I did everything angrily, thumping down the bottles and mixing up the milk roughly. I almost spilled the milk putting the teats on the bottles.

When it was all ready, I carried the two bottles outside

to the calves. The bigger one eagerly butted at the bottle
then drank messily. I held his bottle and at the same time
reached down to my little calf, holding the other bottle
out to him. He didn't seem very interested so I waited
until the first calf had finished, then squatted down with
the weaker one. I held his head to help him get a grip on
the teat. It took a few attempts but finally he seemed to
get the idea. The other calf kept trying to push in but I
shooed him away.

Then I heard a voice. 'That little one'll need a lot of
care.' It was Pa. He lives in the cottage next to our house.
Dad always says he's too old to be of any use on the farm,
but he's Mum's father and she wants him close by so she
can keep an eye on him. He used to be a farmer once
too, and sometimes I think he knows more than Dad. Pa
would never say that, and I wouldn't either. After Mum
and Dad, Pa is my most favourite person in the world.

'Now don't get your hopes up, little fella,' Pa was saying.
'That little calf may not make it. Tell you what, while you're
at school, I'll keep an eye on him for you. Okay?' I hugged
Pa tightly; he always hugs me back. 'You'd better get ready
for school,' he said. 'I'll keep an eye on these two.'

It was an agonizing day at school. I kept thinking
about my calf. I wasn't worried about the stronger one;

he would be fine. But I hoped Pa had been able to check on the little one and sneak in an extra feed if necessary. When Mum picked us up after school, I immediately asked her about the calves.

'Honestly, Sammy, I have no idea. I've been helping Dad all day cleaning the troughs. That's why he trusted you with the calf.'

'With the *calves*,' I corrected her. 'There are two of them.'

She sighed. 'He's a very sick little calf, Sammy. Don't get your hopes up.'

'Well, I am,' I muttered. 'My calf is gonna be okay. I know it.'

This continued for several more days. Whenever I came back from feeding the calf, trying to pretend he was improving and getting stronger, Mum or Dad would sigh and do the same cautious stuff. 'Wait and see how things go,' Mum would say. Even Pa was wary. He was worried I would be disappointed if the calf didn't make it.

One afternoon after school, I walked across to the calves' paddock. The lively one galloped up to greet me. Beside him, on the ground was a white bundle, just like when I first saw my calf. I felt my heart drop somewhere deep inside my chest. Tears were not far away. As usual, I squeezed between the fence wires and knelt beside my calf. His eyes were shut. I called gently to him. No response. Now the tears were starting. My very best friend, my special mate, that Pa and I had looked after so carefully, was dead. I could hardly breathe. I felt like I was choking.

Then I heard Pa's voice. I hadn't heard him approach. 'Sammy boy,' he said, 'look. He knows you're there.'

I strained to see through tears. Everything was blurry. I blinked several times then focused on my little calf. His eyes were open now. He looked at me and I don't really know if calves can smile, but I'm sure he was smiling at me.

He was going to be alright.

Love at First Sight

by Frances Prentice

Long ago I was shiny, my paintwork brand new,
I sat in a showroom, in town,
When in came a young bloke with cash in his hand.
He saw me and slapped it all down.

It was love at first sight for a bloke and his ute,
We drove off up the road with a roar,
Then out on the highway, he opened me up,
With my throttle held down to the floor.

A honeymoon sweet, polished each week,
Not a speck of dirt left on my floor,
We picked up his girl, to take her for a whirl,
Never knowing what next was in store.

The wedding bells rang, as they came down the steps,
Confetti swirled into the air,
I was spruced up a treat for a getaway neat,
Some tin cans applauding our pair.

For the next year or two, they fixed up the nest
And many a hay bale we threw,
To the cattle, so keen, in some country, not green,
Waiting for storms to brew.

Then, with the rain, new life came again,
Young cattle grazing the field,
And his missus, so sweet, also swelled in the heat,
Who knew what the new year would yield?

One day we were out, just poking about,
When we spotted a car with a sign,
A wagon, sedate, sure she'd do for a mate,
So his wife drove her home, that was fine.

Then, with a wail, came a lusty young male,
And I was abandoned – it's true!
They say three's a crowd – with a third one so loud –
I was glad to be built just for two.

But, before long, my mate came with a song
That he whistled while loading my tray,
We were off to cut wood, and provide like we should,
Another young one on the way.

Well, over the years, I saw blood, sweat and tears,
As we scrambled through ditches and scrub,
And my paintwork wore thin, nearly through to the tin,
While my tyres were worn down to the hub.

But we were still mates, the old bloke and I,
And both the boys thought I was beaut,
And when they grew tall, they both had a ball,
In the paddock they'd bash in Dad's ute.

Well, we scraped the odd fencepost, and hit the odd roo,
But a ute is for work, not for looks,
And the dints in my side, they brought their own pride,
The country is no place for sooks.

Then the boys were men, they'd gone off again,
It was just the old codger and me,
But he'd bought a new ute, she was shiny, real beaut,
And he turned me out back, to be free.

Well, I cooked in the sun, and I cried in the rain,
But those skies, what a sight, in the dawn,
And my tyres let go, I just settled, real slow,
Part of the landscape, forlorn.

But then came the day when the grandies did stay,
They dragged Grandad over to see
The rusty old ute that they thought was real beaut
And they played and they played there with me.

Mara and the Mugwump

by Dannielle Viera

The branch wobbled under Mara's feet as her brother skipped along it and leapt into the sky. She peeked past a clump of leaves and watched as Cadi stretched out his four legs and soared to the next tree. 'Come on, Mara,' he yelled. 'You can do it!'

Mara looked down. The ground was so far away! She took one step and then two more. On her fourth step, the branch started to bend. Soon she could feel her toes slipping on the slick surface. With a squeak, she scurried back to the safety of the tree-hollow nest. 'I'm going to fall!' she called out, and then hid her face in her fluffy tail.

A rustle of leaves drew Mara's big black eyes upwards. Mrs Possum sat on the branch above her, nibbling on a plum. 'What's wrong, my dear?' she asked between bites.

'I'm a sugar glider, but I'm too scared to glide,' Mara whimpered.

'Well, that is a problem.' Mrs Possum popped the last piece of plum into her mouth and swallowed. 'Maybe you should talk to the Mugwump. He's the cleverest creature in the bush, so he'll know how to help you.'

Mara sat up, her nose twitching. 'Where can I find him?'

Mrs Possum wiped her whiskers with her paws. 'He lives on an island in the middle of the Great Billabong.'

Mara poked her head out of the tree hollow. Her eyes followed the trunk to the earth below. She'd never set foot on the ground, as Mum had told her and Cadi that it was dangerous. But she wanted to fly like the other sugar gliders. 'I'll do it!' Mara declared, and she scampered down the trunk before she could change her mind.

When she reached the curtain-like roots that swished across the ground before diving beneath the soil, Mara stopped and gazed up. A sea of green rippled in the wind, as birds squawked goodnights and hooted hellos to each other. Around her, the forest floor crackled with unseen life. Strange smells drifted past. Mara rubbed her nose, trying to slow her fluttering heart.

Suddenly, a tiny lizard darted out from a nearby bush.

'Excuse me, do you know the way ...' Mara began to say, but the lizard scuttled off before she could finish her question.

'Are you lost?' rumbled a voice behind her. Mara spun around with a gasp and tumbled off the root. As she lay there, a dark nose surrounded by long whiskers loomed over her. Two eyes blinked from a broad face of brown fur. 'I'm sorry! I didn't mean to frighten you.'

Mara took a deep breath and wriggled back to her feet. 'I'm looking for the Great Billabong.'

The wombat grunted and trundled towards a fern shooting feathery fronds in all directions. Mara sighed and started searching for someone else to help her. 'Well, are you coming?' the wombat asked.

Clicking happily, Mara bounded over to her new friend. The wombat lifted one of the fronds with his head, revealing a narrow path through the undergrowth. 'This trail will take you to the Great Billabong. Be careful, little one.'

'Thank you,' said Mara, and she scooted under the wombat's hairy chin. As she made her way along the track, her feet skidded on slivers of wet bark and sank into piles of rotting leaves. Every so often, she had to scramble over a fallen tree that was covered in slimy moss.

After a while, Mara's tummy began to gurgle. She snuffled around in the leaf litter, trying to find tasty insects. Nearby, a hollow log beckoned. She peered inside ... and jumped back when a forked tongue lashed her nose.

'Hello, sssweetie,' the snake hissed. Scales shimmered black in the twilight as his slender body slid out of the log and slithered in a circle to face her. He lifted his head, exposing a fiery belly.

Mara gulped and tried to sidle under the nearest bush.

'Ssstop! I jussst want to ssspeak to you.' He swayed towards Mara, tongue darting in and out.

Shaking on the spot, Mara scouted around for somewhere to hide. Then she grinned. As the snake's fangs moved closer and closer, Mara bent down. She quickly picked up a stick and smacked the snake on the nose with all the strength she could muster.

'Ow! That hurtsss,' shouted the snake in shock. His food shouldn't fight back! He shook his head and slunk away into the forest.

Mara danced around, waving the stick in the air. A kookaburra laughed from his perch far above her. As the cackle ebbed away, a new sound washed over the scene. *Splish ... splosh ... splash ...*

'That must be an animal playing in the Great Billabong!' cried Mara. Carrying her stick, she dashed in the direction of the noise. Before long, the forest gave way to a muddy bank that sloped towards the water. Trees leaned over the billabong, trying to see their reflection. But the only things they could make out were the first stars of the evening twinkling across the surface. A mob of kangaroos drank their fill, then hopped away.

From the middle of the billabong, an island rose as round and green as a turtle's back. 'How am I going to get over there?' Mara moaned. She walked to the edge of the water, hoping that there would be someone to tell her how to reach the island. Nothing moved except a large piece of bark floating towards her.

As she stared at the bark, a wild idea galloped into her mind. She used her stick to drag the bark closer to her, and then she stepped onto it. Pushing herself across the billabong with the stick, she soon reached the island with a shuddering scrape.

Mara toppled forward off the bark and stood up, quivering. To her left and right, waves lapped gently against the gravelly shore. Bats flew overhead, their wings *whomp, whomp, whomping* across the sapphire sky. Her nose caught a whiff of a weird scent wafting from the centre of the island. It must be the Mugwump!

Threading her way through tall grass, Mara wondered what the Mugwump looked like. Was he kind? Would he help her? Glancing at her coat, she yelped in dismay at her dirty fur. She licked herself as she walked, cleaning off the worst of the mud and slime. By the time she had left the last of the grass behind her, she was almost back to her old self.

In front of her, the ground climbed up to the highest point on the island, where a gum tree teetered in the breeze. And sitting under the tree, surrounded by a crazy collection of critters, was the largest frog that she had ever seen. Mara crept closer.

'We have a visitor,' the Mugwump announced. 'She seems a little ... ruffled.' The other animals turned to gape at Mara, and a mumble hummed through the group.

'H-h-hello S-S-Sir,' Mara stuttered, trying to flatten her scruffy fur. 'I heard that you are the cleverest creature in the bush, so ... I was wondering if you could help me?'

A sticky tongue shot out of the Mugwump's mouth and snatched a bug out of the air. 'Perhaps. What is your problem?'

Mara cleared her throat. 'I ... I ... I'm not brave enough to glide through the sky.'

The Mugwump winked one eye and then the other. 'Codswallop,' he croaked.

'Pardon?' said Mara.

'My flying friends followed every step of your journey, and they told me that you are fearless in the face of danger.'

'That doesn't sound like me,' Mara murmured.

The Mugwump snorted. 'Who boldly left their tree-hollow nest?'

'Me,' replied Mara.

'Who stout-heartedly stood up to a snake?'

'Me,' said Mara with a smile.

'Who courageously crossed the billabong on their own?'

'Me!' shouted Mara, banging her stick on the ground.

The Mugwump puffed out his chest. 'So, what are you going to do now?'

Mara tugged at her tiny whiskers. 'I'm going to glide!'

She cantered through the animals and bolted up the gum tree. Her heartbeats boomed like thunder in her ears. *Don't look down,* she thought as she edged along a high branch. Then, with a squeal, she launched herself from the tree.

As she sailed over the cheering crowd and past the glittery Great Billabong, the wind tickled her toes and smoothed her fur. 'Gliding is so much fun!' Mara hollered happily to the heavens.

New Boot Dreaming

by Kim Horwood

Nⁿew boots. Football boots, with Aboriginal flag design.

Red base, black top, yellow circle. Colours of country, skin, and the sun.

Their red, black and yellow bounced around Daylin's thoughts for half the footy season, like his heart was sick for them. Even when his eyes were closed, he was dreaming of them.

'New boot dreaming,' his Granny told him, 'is a sign of big luck coming.'

Daylin cradled them now in his hands, gently, because holding them too tight might wake him from another dream.

He turned them over and around, stealing their gloss for the glint in his eyes.

He rubbed their shine, that tickled his palms.

He pointed the toe to his nose, breathing them into his belly.

He loosened laces.

Dry calloused feet crept in without socks.

They fantastically hugged his heels, his toes, giving him new anchors to the land. The new boots were light. If he weren't seeing them on his feet, would Daylin even know he had them on? With these boots he would run faster, kick further, leap higher. He'd be deadly.

'Thanks Granny,' Daylin grinned, dabbing eyes with his knuckles because the words tickled his throat. His grandmother had been saving the money from her paintings to buy Daylin's new boots. Every canvas she created was unique, because the women in this part of the country had their own style. Granny's dot-paintings told stories of skin names, country, and connection. When Daylin sat with her, she'd tell him Dreamtime stories while he passed her colours – horizon pink, wattle yellow, sunset gold, spinifex green, fire orange, sky grey.

'Remember, it's your spirit makes you great – not boots,' Granny smiled, her arm soft around his shoulder.

Daylin had never owned a pair of football boots. Before now he preferred bare feet, so country and ochre dust could settle between his toes. From a remote community outside Alice Springs, his footy team the Saints, trained on red dirt field, not expecting to make the grand final. The more games they won, the more people turned out to watch them train. The untouched dust on a five-rung grandstand was now wiped clean by bottoms. It didn't take many people to fill the grandstand, so others leaned on the oval's warm steel fence or sat on bonnets of cars parked front-on so when the sun left, headlights kept training going. Mums and Grans came with snacks, while Dads came with kangaroo tails. They made fires beyond the grandstand and cooked roo and sweet potato in the coals when footy training finished. The community police officer high-fived the team wearing a paper neck chain made by kids at the school, in the Saint's colours, black and red. More black and red paper chains were streamers above heads as kids leapt over blonde grass at the oval's edge, camp dogs nipping at their heels.

Daylin watched the people's faces, their smiling eyes, cheeks bulging with sweet potato, lips disappearing into grins. He admired his feet, ochre dust on shiny black, red and yellow, and his belly fluttered. Not because he was hungry for roo tail, but because his spirit was moved by black and red paper chains, fireside faces, and the hopeful land beneath new boots.

*

Camp dogs chased bus wheels to the dirt road as it carried the Saints on their eighty kilometre grand-final journey to Alice Springs. It was the same mini-bus that picked up kids on school days, not because school was a long way but for those who wanted the Tuckshop's early morning warm milk Milo. The cheeky camp dogs would nip at bus wheels all the way to the school gate, where they'd laze until the last bell then chase the bus home again.

The dog's yaps faded in Daylin's ears as his quiet gaze settled on spinifex, red sand and gidgee trees. Low bushes burst with cheers of surprised speedy finches, as a mob of scruffy brumbies ran proudly with the bus on the outskirts of town. Daylin could smell the red dust burrowed in their straggly manes. Even with boots cradled in his lap, the country filled his spirit through eyes, ears and nose.

On the sideline of a sandy footy field with patchy grass tufts, the Saints laced boots filled with hope. Strapping tape coloured for pink skin was wound around Daylin's wrists. He wrote on the tape in black pen, words that stirred his spirit.

Country.

Skin brothers.

Granny.

Midway through the second quarter, Daylin's shoulders slumped as the scoreboard weighed heavily for the opposition. His spirit fading of brumbies pride and finches speed, Daylin's kicks ricocheted off the edge of glossy new boots, missing their mark.

He dug the toe of his boots at dust between grass tufts. Hands on hips, Daylin panted breath that was hot with defeat. Granny rubbed her frown as the umpire's whistle blew against their team again and again.

At half time Daylin padded barefoot to Granny, his new boots in his hands. Before taking the boots with a nod and a straight lipped smile, she reminded him, 'Spirit makes you great.'

With red dust now between his toes Daylin flew into the wind and over the shoulders of the opposition like a hovering eagle, marking balls higher than he'd ever gone. From the seventy-yard line, his bare feet kicked distances like never before, balls soaring between towering upright posts. Two other players looked at each other then released their feet, tossing their boots to the sideline.

Minutes from full time, the Saints were a goal away from a grand final win. Daylin stopped for a moment to watch faces frozen by the field umpire's stopwatch. Pouted mouths stretched with hope, eyes were wide with promise. Daylin's eyes scanned the mountain range that wrapped the shoulders of town, and then followed the crisscrossed tracks around him in the ochre sand. He nodded to the ancestors whose spirit stirred his belly. Knees bent, he stamped his heal to the ground in readiness for a corroboree, the mountain range his bora ring. Daylin decided this would be a dance like no one had ever seen before.

Granny faced the sun, her eyes closed, as a whirly-whirly spun from the edge of the field, twirling red dust across it's centre.

*

As the school's mini-bus shuddered along the dirt road home, Daylin spied an eagle hovering on a golden sunset. The silhouette of the desert landscape rose from the ochre dust and settled softly. Daylin ran his thumb down his tongue and rubbed dust from the toe of his boots and frowned. His eyes were drawn to the words in black on his wrists.

Country.

Skin brothers.

Granny.

*

'I thought they'd make me play better,' Daylin stared at the boots resting now beside his feet, glossy against dull grey concrete. Granny sat next to him on the verandah couch, nodding but not speaking. Instead she offered him a piece of damper taken from an iron pot sitting in the coals of the fire.

The balls of Granny's cheeks shone with a smile as the warm smell of damper filled Daylin's nostrils. His skin prickled with a thought as sudden as a bush full of surprised finches.

In the same way his Granny's spirit was in the comforting warmth of damper, Daylin realised his spirit was in the ochre dust of the whirly-whirly, the soaring eagle on the horizon, and the proud brumby that tramped the desert trails. He *was* the connection to country, his

skin brothers, and to the wisdom of a respected elder –
his Granny.

'You gotta connect to country, that's what makes ya
better,' Granny said, as if she'd heard his thoughts.

Daylin's heart beat in time with the quiet rhythm of
the wind as he took the damper from Granny's hand.
The breeze on his skin reminded him of the windy final
minutes of the game, when he kicked a goal, then broke
away, his bare feet kicking a point that won the grand
final for the Saints.

'Spirit makes you great,' Granny winked and Daylin
decided too, that she was just as cheeky as those old
camp dogs.

Oh Dear, Oh My, a Drop Bear

by Karen Hendriks

Dusk was creeping. Shadows sprinkled and spread across the forest floor as Willa Woylie sniffed the air. She sent the soil flying everywhere on her truffle hunt, digging deep into a carpet of leaves when...

Plonk!

Phiff!

A startled Willa Woylie let off a fart bomb and made a quick getaway. She hopped off into the bush at great speed. Swish, swish, swish— she was as fast as the wind.

'Hey Willa Woylie! Where're you going in such a hurry?' asked Pip Possum.

'There's a drop bear round here,' said Willa Woylie.

'Then I'd better come too,' said Pip Possum.

And off they hopped and bounded in the forest in the deep dark night until they met Sami Sugar Glider.

'G'day, g'day, Willa Woylie and Pip Possum where're you going in such a hurry?' asked Sami Sugar Glider.

'There's a drop bear round here,' said Willa Woylie.

'We're getting far away,' said Pip Possum.

'I'd better come too,' said Sami Sugar Glider.

And off they hopped and bounded and glided in the forest in the deep dark night until they met Gilbert Potoroo.

G'day, g'day, where're you going in such a hurry?' asked Gilbert Potoroo.

'There's a drop bear round here,' said Willa Woylie.

'We're getting far away,' said Pip Possum.

'They drop from trees,' said Sami Sugar Glider.

'Hmmmm,' pondered Gilbert Potoroo. 'That's frightening. I'd better come too.'

And off they hopped and bounded and glided and bounced in the forest in the deep dark night until they met Spotty Quoll.

'G'day, g'day, Willa Woylie and Pip Possum and Sami Sugar Glider and Gilbert Potoroo, where're you going in such a hurry?' asked Spotty Quoll.

'Oh, Spotty Quoll,' they replied. 'There's a drop bear round here, it's best to get far away because they drop from trees.'

'You can't see 'em,' said Spotty Quoll. 'I'd better come too.'

And off they hopped and bounded and glided and bounced and zipped in the forest in the deep dark night until they met Foxy Fox.

'G'day, g'day, Willa Woylie and Pip Possum and Sami Sugar Glider and Gilbert Potoroo and Spotty Quoll; where're you going in such a hurry?'

'Oh, Foxy Fox,' they replied. 'There's a drop bear round here, so it's best to get far away because they drop from trees and you can't seem 'em.'

'Oh deary me,' said Foxy Fox, grinning. 'It's best you come along with me to the ravine. Drop bears can't cross over but we can.'

Willa Woylie and Pip Possum and Sami Sugar Glider and Gilbert Potoroo and Spotty Quoll followed Foxy Fox to the edge of the ravine.

'How do we get across, Foxy Fox?' they all asked.

'We go over that log,' he replied.

'It's wibbly, wobbly and itty bitty,' said Willa Woylie.

'It might tip into the ravine,' said Pip Possum.

'We'll all be too heavy if we cross at once,' said Sami Sugar Glider.

'I'm not sure it's safe,' said Gilbert Potoroo.

'It's a long way down,' said Spotty Quoll.

'Don't be ridiculous. You're all scaredy cats! Just watch me,' said Foxy Fox.

Foxy Fox edged his way across the log over the deep dark ravine and once he was in the middle he called, 'Follow me now.'

No one was too keen. There was a squibble and a squabble between Willa Woylie and Pip Possum and Sami Sugar Glider and Gilbert Potoroo and Spotty Quoll about who would go first. Then, just as they all turned around, a drop bear appeared in the tree above the ravine.

Kerplonk!

That drop bear landed upon the edge of the log over the deep dark ravine and sent Foxy Fox flying through the air to land with a Kersplat! Foxy Foxy was way down below at the bottom of the ravine.

'I'll get you all for this!' he cried.

'There's a drop bear round here, and it's best to get far away because they drop from trees and they're hard to see and they're scary,' they all cried.

Then quick as a Willa Woylie stink they all spun around and hopped and bounded and glided and bounced and zipped their way back into the forest where they'd come from on this deep dark night. They were back home in bed before the crack of dawn.

Each one was left wondering if they'd really been saved from the razor-sharp teeth of Foxy Fox by a drop bear that had completely disappeared. Or had it all been imagined?

On the Farm

by Maura Pierlot

My cousins were coming to visit our farm.
Just city meets country, no need for alarm.
The moment I heard a loud engine, then doors,
I ran out the back and abandoned my chores.

'We're finally here! That car trip was too long,'
my cousins insisted, and they were not wrong.
Out came the esky, their bags and a ball,
a cricket set, longboards then more gear to haul.

'Hey, where are the sheep?' all my cousins did ask.
To them, sheep are toys, but for us they're a task.
'They're out in the paddock,' I said, 'near the shed.'
'You're shearing?' they blurted and ran off ahead.

My dad had just finished his last shearing run
and put down his handpiece to greet everyone.
Sweat dripped down his brow as some beaded on mine.
My auntie just smiled, said the heat was 'divine'.

'You hungry?' Dad asked, 'I can round up a lamb,
or pig,' he suggested, 'if you prefer ham.'
The mouths on my cousins dropped down to their chins
with awkward new thoughts about how meat begins.

Then just as the sun was beginning to set,
'Tomorrow, the mowing!' Mum said, 'don't forget!'
The eyes of my cousins popped open real wide
at grass all around, the far acres they spied.

'You mow with a ride-on? We'll help you, okay?
But not with a push one, we'd be here all day.'
I wanted to trick them but had too much heart.
'The sheep eat all that, we just mow this one part.'

'Thank goodness,' they shouted, as Mum called out, 'Tea!'
'That's dinner,' I told them, 'smells good, but we'll see.'
We washed our hands twice before taking a seat.
The veggies were served and then two types of meat.

The looks on their faces showed dread and dismay,
my cousins unable to find words to say.
They eyed our new dog, hoping she'd snatch the meat.
But there was too much for a young pup to eat.

'Remember your visit,' they asked, 'just last year?'
How could I forget such a strange atmosphere?
'I'd never seen so many cars,' I explained,
'and people and pets in one city, contained.'

And right in that moment I knew we're the same.
When out of our comfort zone, no one's to blame.
I looked at their meat, which I snuck for my plate.
But ate it too quickly and needed to wait.

I munched on their ham then I took a third chop.
They smiled as I chewed. There was no time to stop.
My cousins' jaws dropped and their eyes opened wide.
Their plates were now empty with no food to hide.

'My my, you're good eaters,' Mum said to us all.
'Have some more meat so you'll grow nice and tall.'
'No, no!' I cried out. There was no time to waste.
I had eaten so much, my taste buds couldn't taste.

'We need to save room for dessert,' I tricked Mum.

She nodded, amazed we could fit in a crumb.

And then I remembered, they're here for the week.

Six more cousin dinners – a meat-eating streak!

Once Upon a Billabong

by Norah Colvin

Once upon a billabong way out west,
Sat a great big bullfrog boasting he was best.
Along came another, seeking shelter for the night,
Last thing he wanted was a ding-dong fight.

'Hey!' said the bully frog, puffing out his chest.
'Ya can't sleep here — find another place to rest.'
The other one looked sideways, then gave a timid smile.
'I'm sure to be no bother. I'll only stay a while.'

'One, and one night only, then you must be on your way.
You'll have to find an empty pond, a place where you can stay.'
'But all the ponds are drying up, the earth is parched and brown.'
'That's not my concern,' said Bully Frog. 'Go find yourself a town.'

And so, it happened time again, travellers asked to stay,
But every time, ungraciously, they were rudely sent away.
He didn't care their homes were burnt or knocked down to
the ground.
It wasn't his fault ever if no other homes were found.

'This is my pond only,' he bragged and puffed his chest.
Even if someone challenged and put him to a test.
The frog became notorious, the meanest of the mean.
And soon they all avoided him. He was left alone to preen.

Then giant machines came roaring, tearing up the earth,
Unwinding coils of black snakes of monumental girth.
They sucked up all the water and left the pond so dry
That even bully bullfrog could only sit and cry.

He croaked and croaked and croaked so loud, he thought his
heart would burst.
Machines don't care or even know which one of you was first.
That didn't stop the bully frog raising up a fist.
He took a swipe. For all it did, he may as well have missed.

Without a drop of water left and nothing else to do
He packed his bags and hit the road, a lonely traveller too.
Tired and sore he came upon somewhere he thought to stay
But each door opened, quickly closed and he was sent away.

'You're not welcome,' went the chorus. 'You wouldn't let us stay.
Now, you're the one who's homeless and we're the ones who say.
There's no room here for meanness, and something you will find
Our community thrives on friendship and treating others kind.'

The bully frog he hung his head and started heading out.
He'd not gone far when he was stopped when someone gave a
shout.
'Hey, bully frog, you think that you could change your ways today?
Could you treat others kindly and in a friendly way?'

Now bully frog had walked all day and he was tuckered out.
He wanted somewhere he could sleep, that was without a doubt.
He nodded yes but someone said, 'I think he might be scheming.'
Another said, 'No, he can't stay, tell him we think he's dreaming.'

'I promise,' said the bully frog. 'Cross my heart and hope to die.
Give me a chance and I will do all that I can to try.'
The others found a comfy spot where bully frog could rest.
'Thank you,' said the bully frog. 'You really are the best.'

From that day forth the bully frog became one of the team.
No more a bully frog, he turned into a green.
And together all the animals united one for one
Until the battle for the bush was over, done and won.

Peek-A-Boo Echidna

by Sandra Bennett

'Here come the humans. Quick, on the count of three, 1, 2, 3, hide!' Joey bounced across the paddock to hop head-first into his mummy's pouch. His hind legs dangled out of the top. He tried to squeeze them in, but he had almost outgrown her pouch. He couldn't tuck them in any further. Mummy tried to kick him out, again he refused to budge.

Wombat scurried to dig a hole under a fallen tree trunk. Dirt scattered in a flurry as his claws scrambled to dig deep enough to squeeze under. His bottom stuck out a little bit. If he didn't move, maybe they wouldn't notice.

Koala scuttled up the nearest gum tree to reach shelter among the thickest leaves that formed a canopy. She hoped she was camouflaged enough in the mottled sunlight.

Echidna waddled to and fro. He didn't know where to

hide in such a hurry. He tucked his little head under his tummy, turned himself into a spikey ball and froze in the middle of the paddock. If he didn't move, and kept his head safely tucked under, he couldn't see the humans, and they would never see him.

Echidna listened. The vibrations on the ground grew closer. Were the humans seeking prey, like the cunning fox that often crossed their path? He popped his head out for a quick glance. Then tucked himself back into a tight ball.

'Peek-a-boo, Echidna, we can see you,' a voice laughed from above. A hand gently stroked his spikes so that he relaxed, just a little.

'You are a brave little echidna. We aren't going to hurt you.'

Echidna peeked out from under his tummy. There were several pairs of dirt scuffed boots surrounding him. He didn't dare move. He stayed frozen in the middle of the paddock while voices above laughed and chatted.

After a while, he felt more vibrations rumble through his body. Echidna poked his head out and opened his eyes to watch the humans walk away. He was a brave echidna. He had stood his ground and survived to tell his friends about his encounter.

Holding his head high, Echidna waddled across the paddock, found the safety of a low bush, dug a hole just big enough underneath, snuggled in and fell fast asleep.

The ground shook, Echidna woke startled to smell smoke. The air was a thick yellow haze. It stung his eyes and made it hard to breathe. An uneasy lump grew in the pit of his tummy. The ground rumbled as a kangaroo mob bounded out of the bush, through the open field and disappeared somewhere into the haze. He caught a glimpse of Joey hopping desperately to keep up. Joey's leaps were not near big enough. He called out to his mummy. In a flash, she turned, raced back, scooped up her little joey and was gone.

Echidna searched for Koala. Where was she? Each time he called out for her, his throat grew drier, his voice became hoarse. He scurried from the base of one tree to the next, someone must have still been around. Where were they all hiding?

'Peek-a-boo, Echidna, I see you,' Koala climbed down the trunk of a gumtree, but Echidna's relief didn't last long. 'Fire,' Koala pointed. 'The bush is on fire. It's burning fast and it's coming our way. Run.' Koala then scampered back up the tree trunk.

'Aren't you coming?' Echidna trembled. He didn't want to be left alone.

'No, I'll be fine, I can climb out of the way. Go now, before it's too late.' Koala then scrambled higher into the tree and disappeared among the leaves and branches.

Day became night as the smoke blackened out the sun. Echidna darted across the paddock after the mob of kangaroos. He knew he had no hope catching them but maybe he could find Wombat. As he reached the next group of trees a head poked out from under a fallen log.

'Peek-a-boo, Echidna I see you.' Echidna's heart skipped a beat. Wombat was calling him. 'Over here,' Wombat herded Echidna towards the log. 'The opening to my burrow is just under here. It winds long and deep underground. You'll be safe in here with me until the fire passes.'

Echidna gladly followed Wombat into the tunnel, the further down he waddled, the darker and cooler it became. The smoke and heat didn't seem to have reached down here. When Echidna felt his little legs couldn't carry him any further, the tunnel opened into Wombat's home. The burrow was cosy and inviting, eucalypt leaves carpeted the floor, in the far corner lay a soft bed of petals. A string of gumnuts decorated the cavern wall. Echidna released one final shiver and let his spikes relax. He joined Wombat on the pile of petals and allowed his eyes to close.

Echidna woke to dust filling the air. He forgot where he was and started to panic.

'Fire, the fire is here, we're trapped,' Echidna circled the floor, scattering leaves. He stopped and tucked his head under his tummy to turn into a tight spiky ball.

'Calm down,' laughed Wombat. 'Sorry about that, the fire can't get in here. I had an itch I had to scratch. The billowing dust was just me rubbing my behind against the wall.' Echidna poked out his head, sniffed the air to be sure then gave a little shake.

'I suppose I did overreact. Do you think it's safe to go outside yet?'

'Only one way to find out,' Wombat rubbed his butt against the wall one last time and sighed. 'Let's go.' He meandered back into the tunnel and vanished.

Echidna's tummy was rumbling, the hunger pains almost overcame his fear to peek outside. He decided if Wombat went first, it would be okay to follow. The closer they came to the end of the tunnel, the more he could smell smoke as it wafted through the entrance. Maybe this wasn't such a good idea after all.

Wombat stopped, Echidna bumped into him and fell backwards. He hadn't expected that. He squeezed up beside Wombat and together they peered out from under the singed log. It and the ground were black and smouldering. The orange haze had turned grey as steam sizzled from tree trunks and branches. A drop of water plopped onto Echidna nose as he crept forward out of the safety of Wombat's home. A strange red powder ran in a wide line across the paddock. The ground didn't seem to be as burnt on the other side. He couldn't help it, curiosity enticed him for a closer sniff.

As Echidna waddled forward, his paws began to hurt, the black dirt was hot beneath his paws, the pads on his paws began to burn. He reached out to touch the red powder. It was soft and cooler underfoot. As Echidna glanced around his burnt and charred home the ground rumbled beneath him again. Instinctively he tucked himself into a spiky ball and froze on the spot.

'Peek-a-boo, Echidna we see you. It's okay, you're safe now.' A gloved hand reached down to carefully pick him up. As Echidna opened his eyes, the same dusty boots from before surrounded him, but this time they too, were blackened. 'Don't fret little one, we are here to take you to a safe place where we can look at your sore feet. Then when the fire is over and it's safe to return, we'll bring you back home.'

Just before Echidna's eyes were covered as he slipped into a soft, cosy human-made pouch, he spied Koala in the arms of one of the humans. Koala snuggled in and clung tight. The human offered a water bottle to Koala and she lapped it up. Another human held a branch of fresh gum leaves for her. If Koala felt safe, Echidna decided he must be safe now too. Maybe the humans weren't so bad after all. He would be happy to go with them. He would be a brave Echidna, and wouldn't he have a grand adventure to tell Wombat and Joey when he and Koala returned.

Plating up

by David Perkins

My eyes had fallen on the ad
As I opened the paper.
An artist's competition,
That seemed a likely caper.

I cast ajar my cupboard door,
The world heard my complaint.
I found no sheet of canvas,
Nor even tube of paint.

Not to be discouraged,
I took a needled thread
And sewed myself together
Several bits of bread.

'This shall be my canvas sheet,'
I was heard to utter.
'And for light yellow pigment
I shall use unsalted butter.'

For verdant hues of hills so green,
For each rain forest valley,
I shall dab upon my canvas
A jar of fresh mint jelly.

For crimson red the only choice
Was obvious of-course.
I chose to render scarlet
With some red tomato sauce.

With cream I made a pallid hue
To whiten up my print.
For grey I used my belly button
And fossicked for some lint.

For an amber sun I made a circle
And refrained from spending money
By rendering the solar orb
With a dab of blue gum honey.

Another problem I was facing,
A rather tricky one,
Was how to stop the local flies
From orbiting my sun?

One colour proved not easy,
A most complicated hue.
The conundrum placed before me was...
How would I make blue?

Blueberries are not blue enough,
They're purple if you please.
The source of blue I came upon
Were the veins in blue-vein cheese.

I gathered it all together
And put in on the deck,
Then packed it my backpack
And set off on a trek.

To seek the perfect place to stand
From which to paint my art,
Australia's whitest beaches?
Or its regal blood red heart?

I dreamed of Namatjira
And Nolan with their skill.
I tried to channel McCubbin
To find that perfect hill.

Then I found that flawless spot
With a campfire and a creek
And a mountain in the background.
It should only take a week.

At last my work was finished,
My opus was complete.
At least it didn't look as though
I made it with my feet.

I packed it in a carton
And sent it off that day
And waited for the judges' word
To see what they would say.

Finally, soon after that,
I received a prompt reply
As I opened up the missive
With hope still in my eye.

Sadly though, my painting vanished!
The judges couldn't rate it.
It seems that when it had arrived
The adjudicators ate it.

The letter I'm holding now,
This epistle sent to me,
Isn't telling me I've won,
But they want the recipe.

Postcard from the Outback

by Lorraine Halse

It was an extremely hot day in January, and we were on a holiday in the Australian Outback. I counted the road signs as we passed them. I watched as the scenery changed from flat, barren land to thick clusters of dry woody Mulga. We had been on the road for several hours. 'It must have been 45 degrees outside,' I thought to myself. There seemed to be no life outside our car. I asked Mum if anything lives out here. 'It's too hot for the animals to come out during the day,' Mum replied. 'They wait until it cools down late in the afternoon or early in the morning.'

Mum stopped the car in the shade of a tree to have a cuppa and stretch her legs. I grabbed some Anzac biscuits for afternoon tea and walked into the bush. I dropped a biscuit and as I looked down, a goanna picked it up in his long, sharp claws as if to pass it back to me.

I smiled and said, 'you keep it'. He scurried off into the bush, his tail swaying from side to side. I decided to follow him.

I heard the call of a black and white magpie and looked up. That's when I lost sight of the big goanna. I followed the magpie as she flew to a gum tree in the distance. I watched as she fed her chicks in the nest. I whistled to her as I put some biscuit crumbs on a rock nearby. As I walked away, she swooped down to the rock. She bowed her head as if to say thank you. I smiled.

I heard a rustle in the dry spinifex and watched quietly as a family of hopping mice darted from one bush to another. It seemed strange to see them during the day. Maybe I disturbed them? I threw a few crumbs towards them. They seemed to smile at me as they nibbled the crumbs and left as quickly as they came.

I sat on a rock to tie my shoelace when I saw a scorpion. It blended into the colour of the dirt which made it hard to see. It had a long tail with a point on the end and two long pincers. I don't think it saw me as it scurried by on its way to who knows where.

This was my first visit to the Outback. We were going to visit Mum's brother, my Uncle. He lives on a cattle station. He usually visits us in the city, and I was looking forward to seeing him again. He said he would teach me how to ride a horse!

It was time to head back to the car. I wasn't sure how far I'd come or how long I'd been gone. I had left the path and now felt lost. I stood still and looked around. I could see the tree with the magpie's nest and walked towards it. I had finished my biscuits and was thirsty. I wished I had my water bottle with me.

I wasn't watching where I walked and tripped over a fallen branch. As I got to my feet, I saw a snake slithering away from me. I did not know what sort of snake it was, and I wasn't going to follow it! I regained my balance and as I did, I saw the path. I felt a sigh of relief.

I could see Mum in the distance, walking towards me. I ran to her and hugged her tight. 'I'm sorry I wandered off without you Mum,' I said, 'I promise not to do it again'. Mum hugged me back and handed me my water bottle knowing that I would be thirsty by now.

I told Mum about the birds and animals I'd seen. Mum smiled at me as we jumped in the car and set off on our journey to the Cattle Station.

It was late afternoon and we began to see the tall red Kangaroos with joeys in their pouches eating the small grass that grew along the side of the road.

We saw an emu running alongside the barbed wire fence as if to race the car. It was a funny sight indeed.

I must have dozed off because the next thing I knew my Uncle was calling my name as he opened the car door. It was dark and I could see the lights were on in the homestead. There was a fire with people sitting around it. Someone was playing a guitar and others were singing. I smiled back at my Uncle. At that moment I saw an owl swoop down and collect something from the ground.

It was our first day and I had already experienced so much of the land and the wildlife, I couldn't wait to send a postcard to my friends and tell them all about it.

Septic Tank Swim Team

by Annaleise Byrd

The smell hits me as soon as I get off the school bus. The septic tank guy must be at our house today. I flick my ponytail over my shoulder and trudge up the driveway, breathing through my mouth. It doesn't work—the smell seeps in through my tonsils instead.

All day, I've been desperate to get home and play with our kittens. Our farm cat, Mischief, has three this time. They're eight weeks old, and they sleep in a box on our back verandah. I know my time with them is running out—Mum's already put an ad in the paper to give them away—so I've been playing with them as much as possible. But the septic stench puts me off that idea today.

City kids wouldn't know about septic tanks. When they flush the toilet, the contents get whisked away to the water treatment plant and they never have to think about it again. Easy peasy.

But country kids... well, we know it only goes as far as the small concrete tank sunk into our backyard. Sure, the bacteria in the tank do their thing, but the goopy stuff at the bottom still needs pumping out every year or two. I probably don't need to tell you where the watery stuff goes. There's a reason the grass is always greenest around the septic tank.

When I reach the house, Dad and the septic tank guy are chatting beside the truck. The lid's already off the tank—that explains the smell—but they haven't started pumping yet. I give them a wave then hightail it inside.

Mum's in the kitchen. She hands me a snack and asks about my day. Then she breaks the news. 'A lady called about my ad, Janey. She's coming to look at the kittens in an hour.'

I drop my snack and run outside. I don't want to waste a single minute. Only an hour left with the kittens! I'll just have to put up with the smell.

I hurry to their box in the corner of the verandah.

They're not there.

I look around, checking all the usual spots. They're not lapping at their milk bowl. They're not napping on the path. They're not scampering around the clothesline.

Then I hear it. A tiny 'mew'.

And two more. 'Mew! Mew!'

I look further into the backyard. Mischief is standing on top of the septic tank, her tail twitching worriedly. She's looking down at something. Something in the middle of the septic tank. The round lid of the tank is lying in the lush grass nearby.

I sprint over. I stare down through the opening. At first, all I see is a circle of oily brown sludge, surrounded by shadow.

Then they paddle into view. 'Mew! Mew! Mewww!'

'MUM!' I shriek. 'DAD! THE KITTENS ARE IN THE SEPTIC TANK!'

Mum erupts from the house. Dad and the septic tank guy rush over. The four of us—plus Mischief—gaze down into the tank as the three kittens doggy-paddle around their porridge-y pool of poo.

For a moment, we're all frozen.

Then Mischief dips an experimental paw through the opening. She pulls her paw back.

'A board!' Dad gasps. He runs off towards the shed.

Mum wrings her hands. 'Gloves!' she exclaims, dashing

back into the house.

The septic tank guy just stares into the hole with his mouth hanging open.

'Mew! Mew! Mewww!'

I can't stand it any longer. I don't care about the smell. I don't care about the poo. I don't care about my white school shirt. I only care about the kittens.

I lie down on my stomach, my head over the hole. I reach into the tank, trying not to gag.

The black-and-white kitten swims towards me. I pinch the scruff of his neck and pluck him out of the sludge. He curls up, and I plop him into the grass beside the tank.

I lean over the hole again. I grab the ginger kitten. I lift her out of the tank and place her beside her brother. Mischief sniffs them, but doesn't seem to know what else to do.

Mum and Dad return, rubber gloves and wooden board in hand. I smile smugly to myself. I'm doing fine without them. I haven't even got any poo on my fingers.

I reach into the tank one more time. The little tabby kitten is paddling around the edge, almost out of reach. She's going at an awesome pace. She'd be unbeatable in the Cat Olympics. I lean in as far as I dare.

'Janey, use this!' Dad tries to angle the board through

the hole. It catches my ponytail. The ends of my hair splash down into the poo. I jerk my head up. My slimy ponytail flicks across my mouth.

'BAURGH!' I spit.

I try to sit up. My hand misses the edge of the hole. I flop sideways, hitting my shoulder on the rim. My arm splashes down into the tank.

The little supercharged swim champ crashes into my arm. I scoop her up. I struggle upright and cuddle her to my chest.

For a moment, there's silence.

Then Dad and the septic tank guy break into applause. Mum flaps the gloves weakly and mumbles something about my white school shirt. Then she starts clapping too.

I have poo in my hair. Poo in my mouth. Poo up my arm. My shoulder hurts. I stink. And I feel like a hero.

***

An hour later, the lid is back on the tank. The truck has gone. The posh city lady who comes for the kittens likes the little tabby one the best. She cradles her against her cheek and inhales her fluffy, freshly-shampooed fur. She raves on and on about how fantastic she smells.

'I'll take her,' she says. 'But how did you get her to smell so amazing?'

I shrug. 'Just fresh country air,' I say. And I kiss the little tabby goodbye.

She'll Be Right

by Warwick O'Neill

'She'll be right. It's only water.' Percy Dodds proclaimed,
As the flood rushed through 'Calamity Downs' after months of
  pouring rain.
The wheat crop's just been flattened, mere days before the harvest,
Sheep and cattle crowd the higher ground where the dirt is at its
  hardest.
'The fences will all need fixin' and the shearin' sheds gone South,
But at least the water level's only halfway up the house.
We've got tucker to keep us going for at least a couple of days
But I don't mind sayin' fellas, I'll be happy to see some rays.'

'She'll be right, they're only insects' said Percy undismayed.
As swarms of locusts ravaged his crops, at least five on every blade.
A fresh new crop had risen, things were looking pretty good.
Now there's only stubble, where lush green fields once stood.

'Well I suppose they're entitled to a feed, as all things in nature are.
Won't be long and they'll be gone, to some other paddock afar.
I reckon we'll get a crop next year, if me usual good luck will stay.
But I don't mind sayin' fellas, I'll be happy when the bugs go away.'

'She'll be right, it's just a bit dry.' Percy told those gathered round
As the wind blew up a willy willy from the parched and grassless
ground.
The flood is just a memory, three years since they last saw rain
They wonder as they kick the dust, will we ever see it again.
'The sheep are a bit on the thin side and the dairy cows just give dust,
Been so long since we put in a crop, the plough's begun to rust.
The chooks have gone off layin' and the sheep dog's got the mange.
But I don't mind sayin' fellas, I'll be happy to see a change.'

'She'll be right, it's just a fire.' Percy turned around to shout
As fire raged through the Mallee scrub, bone dry from years of drought.
Embers fly on cyclone winds sparking fires far and near
The stockyards, fences and shearing shed gone, and we've lost the
saddle gear.
'Don't worry about the fences, they were no good when they went in.
And as for that flamin' shearing shed, it was built from scraps of tin.
The ground is scorched, the cart is torched, the trees all burnt and
blackened.

But I don't mind sayin' fellas, I'll be happy when the fire slackens. '

'She'll be right, though times are tough.' Percy mumbled to his beer.
Prices low, the market's dropped, it's the same thing year on year.
Through flood and drought and fire and all sorts of things
alarming
Takes a special breed in Australia to do this thing called farming.
'The Bank's been sendin' letters of a really threatenin' nature.
Demandin' money for this and that, and making threats of forfeiture.
I'd really like to please 'em but there's nothin' in me purse,
But I don't mind sayin' fellas, I reckon me Old Man had it worse.'

Spud

by Warwick O'Neill

We lobbed into the Isa on our trip around the state,
To say g'day to a couple of mates we haven't seen in years.
To enjoy a campfire and a cook up, and of course a couple
o' beers.

While we sat there yakkin' I heard a threatenin' growl,
As I looked back behind my seat my amusement began
to grow.
'Cause there he was, a shaggy dog guardin' his potato.

Weren't nuthin' really special 'bout this particular spud.
He'd pulled it from the compost heap, and had emerged
smellin' bloody feral.
But to him that spud was pure gold, you'd take it at your
peril.

It was his mate that came to investigate, that elicited that growl.

But his mate came even closer, and so he nipped him good an' hard,

Then took the spud between his teeth and buried it in the yard.

Now you'd reckon by next morning, he'd have forgot 'bout that spud.

But as we loaded up and said 'hoo roo' we heard the growl one more,

And sure enough dog and spud were sittin' at the door.

Now I know I lack the lyrical skills of Henry Lawson, the "Breaker" or Banjo.

Nor have I got the philosophical bent of Aristotle, Socrates or Plato,

But I thought I might pen a little verse about a dog and his bloody potato.

Taking the Short Cut to School

by Carolyn Foreman

Photos today. No time for play.
Have to get ready for school.

Shoes, tick. Socks, tick.
Pants and shirt and hat, tick.

Homework in the bag, tick.
Not a minute to lose.

Face, tick. Hands, tick.
Teeth and ears and hair, tick.

Check the smile. Double tick.
Okay ready to move.

Zoom out the gate. Mustn't be late.
Can't wait for the bus. Too slow.

Race out the back. Hit the dirt track.
Short cut's the smart way to go.

Over the tyres. Under the wires.
Only a bit of a squeeze.

Whoops double back. Bull on the track.
Definitely not looking pleased.

Bolt to the creek. No rain this week.
Easily make it across.

Whoops mid-air crash. Only a splash.
Bag isn't much of a loss.

Tear round the bend. Bull back again.
Whoops I might have been spotted.

Shin up the tree. Mulberries are free.
Stash a few in the pocket.

Cutting it fine. Bell goes at nine.
Pig pen's the quickest way through.

Whoops bit of muck. Not all bad luck.
Faster with only one shoe.

Hurdle the rail. Whoops spiky nail.
Lucky the undies are new.

Skid down the hill. Whoops little spill.
Cows must have come this way too.

Brush off the dirt. Tuck in the shirt.
Have to be looking my best.

Zoom in the gate. Not even late.
Teacher looks pretty impressed.

Clean up the face. Jump into place.
Right in the very front row.

Slick down the hair. Seconds to spare.
Short cut's the smart way to go.

The Ballad of Meggs Bradford

by Jennifer Horn

It was out in old dry Maryvale
When the train tracks still clacked through,
And the spotted gums would joust the sky,
Lived brothers one, three and two.

The middle was a feisty lad,
A firecrack on legs.
And ginger red upon his head –
T'was why they called him 'Meggs'.

He was the local larrikin,
The schoolyard's Robin Hood.
He'd pick a fight if the words were right
And a mate ain't treated good.

So, the other brothers walked ahead,
To avoid these little clashes.
And Bradford 'Meggs' brought up the rear
In bare feet, pluck and patches.

And out to fetch the daily milk, he'd swing that bucket 'round,
Then fill it up with water so it still weighed by the pound.
His mother'd say, 'Now how 'bout that – that grocerman's got cheek
To think he'll water down our milk – it's happened twice this week!'

But lo, by far the biggest err was the single game of Dare
When pride was prone, and trusts were trussed, and risks beyond repair.
The day that Meggs (as a 'man of the house') went out to chop the wood
And younger brother followed out, as younger brothers could.

That brother lay his finger on the block — 'I dare you chop.'
Well, Meggs thought brother'd move his hand, and brother
thought he'd stop.
So, when the axe came down upon a finger unremoved,
There was a wail! There was a gasp!
Now how can *that* be soothed?

And to this very day, it's true,
That young Meggs' capers linger,
But none were near as bad as when
He chopped off brother's finger.

Endnote:
And though this kid in all his cheek
Was a questionable lad,
He makes for us forevermore
A wonderful Grandad.

The Ballad of Uncle Bill

by Fiona C Lloyd

It was winter at the station on the road to Rusty Hill,
When Sly Jones arrived from Big Smoke to call on Uncle Bill.
He gave a shake and shiver as the cart pulled down the track.
'It's colder here than Big Smoke, but I'm never going back.'

The cart, it rolled and rattled. Sly Jones, he groaned and cried.
The bullocks sniffed and snorted when the driver whipped
their sides.
They jolted over cattle grids, 'til bones ached blue and black.
Then passed through Deadman's graveyard, to the door of
Bill's tin shack.

G'day said Bill, Good day said Sly. They shook each other's hand.
'What brings a bloke like you,' Bill said, 'from Big Smoke to
this land?'
'Perhaps a cup of tea first?' said Sly Jones to Uncle Bill,
'Before we get to matters of my late Aunt Jessie's will'

So, the fire was burnt to ashes and the billy long gone cold,
When Jessie's will had told its tale of how the shack was sold.
And Uncle Bill had countered 'But I won it fair and square,
In a wager with the shearer at the annual country fayre!'

At the crowning of the sunrise, in the shack near Rusty Hill,
Sly Jones awoke to bird song with his stomach all a-thrill
for the new life he'd imagined, when the builders came to town,
And the fun he'd have in Rusty Hill with Uncle's shack pulled
down.

Alone in Deadman's graveyard, where the gum trees mind
the land,
Old Bill sat still with half a tear, and weary head in hand.
The shearer's broken promise, how he'd sold Bill's shack for gold,
Had got him down, and wondering why the shearer'd never told.

But Uncle Bill was more than tear, and more than gold or lie.
And up he jumped and wiped his eye, and gave a battle cry!
And through the bush he tripped and traipsed, with holler, coo
and yell,
For the friends he'd made in Rusty Hill, to take Sly Jones to hell.

Came 'Prickly Joe' echidna, eager emu's, cockatoos,
Magpies, snakes and huntsmen, and a mob of Kangaroos.
They made a plan to help the man they knew as Uncle Bill,
Who had fed them fair and plenty from his shack near Rusty
Hill.

It was two weeks Sunday morning, when the ground was damp
with dew,
That all agreed with hand on heart, the plan had been thought
through.
And one by one they gathered on the road to Rusty Hill,
To send bad Sly a-packing from the house of dear old Bill.

Across the sill the Huntsmen crawled to where Jones lay in bed.
With giant legs and fearful grin across Sly's face he spread.
And Prickly Joe was waiting, spines a-quiver by the door,
To spike the toes of bad Sly Jones, when he jumped from bed
to floor.

The scream Sly Jones emitted could be heard from far and wide.
It gave the signal loud and clear to the animals outside.
And one by one they took their turn to help their dear friend Bill,
To save his shack from bad Sly Jones and Auntie Jessie's will.

They chased him to the graveyard where the bones of men lay
dead,
And begging for his freedom, he repealed the words he'd said.
'Dear Bill old chap, the shack is yours, and I renounce my claim.
Call Kangatoo's and Cockaroo's to end this crazy game.'

'Fair play,' winked Bill, 'my mates and I, we'll miss you all the
same,
But you'd better get a move on to catch that Big Smoke train.'
So, Emu chased Sly down the hill, with belly all a-drum,
And beat the sound that went around, to say that they had won.

My Uncle Bill's been dead and gone for fifty years or more,
But the story of his victory is written on the door.
Of time gone by, since Big Smoke Sly, who came to Rusty Hill.
To steal the shack that mates gave back to my dear old Uncle Bill.

The Blue Tongue who Wanted a Name

by Carolyn Foreman

I'm a blue-tongue lizard who's feeling blue.
I don't have a name of my own like you
Or the boy from the house and his dog and his cat
And his birds and his fish and his mouse and his rat
And the huge hairy spider who hides in his hat.
They all have a name but me.

I live in the wild but I'm really quite tame.
I have all I need but I don't have a name
Like Rocket and Socks and Chirpy and Cheeky
And Orca and Tiger and Squeaky and Sneaky
And even the spider who Harry calls Freaky.
I only want my own name.

The Blue Tongue who Wanted a Name by Carolyn Foreman

I don't want a kennel, a cage or a bowl,

I have my own home in a snug hidey-hole.

I don't want a basket, a box or a bed.

I don't want to play, or be carried or led

Or bathed or brushed or patted or fed.

I only want my own name.

I don't want to go to the park for a run.

I'm happy to bask on the path in the sun

And fossick for snails and slaters and slugs

And spiders and berries and beetles and bugs.

I don't want cuddles or kisses or hugs.

I only want my own name.

I live all alone in a cosy old log,

Safely away from the cat and the dog.

If they come near and I fear they might bite,

I stick out my blue tongue and give them a fright.

I just want to scare them; I don't want to fight.

I only want my own name.

My scales protect me from scratches and scrapes,
Though I have had a couple of lucky escapes.
A crafty old cat once pounced on me
And I dropped my poor tail to set myself free.
It's almost grown back now as you can see.
I only want my own name.

I'm creeping up close to the house today
To sit by the window and watch while they play.
I think I hear footsteps coming around.
I'll have to be quiet; I won't make a sound.
I'll have to be quick; I don't want to be found.
I only want my own name.

I'm deep in a hole but I hear Harry say,
'Hello there Bluey, how are you today?
It's okay Bluey, I'm not coming near.
Don't worry Bluey, there's nothing to fear.
It's okay Bluey, I'm not staying here.
Somebody's calling my name.'

He called me Bluey! He gave me a name!
He called me Bluey and now I'm the same
As you and him and Squeaky and Sneaky
And Orca and Tiger and Chirpy and Cheeky
And Rocket and Socks and huge hairy Freaky.
I'm Bluey. I have my own name.

I'm no longer blue. My wish has come true.
I'm a blue-tongue whose name is Bluey.

The Hitchhiker

by Jennifer Horn

The dropbear sat upon her branch, her tenth leaf chewed that morn,
And all around, her neighbours snored – she looked at them in scorn.
Why bother with koalas? she thought, *They're all so boring.*
They sit and sleep and snore and chew – I want to go exploring!

Then through the scrub there came a noise; raised fur upon her neck —
The sound of cheerful backpackers out on a morning trek,
Their faces fresh and curious to see Australia-wide.
Those humans — they go hitchhiking, she thought. *I'll hitch a ride.*

She landed on a Dutchman; his name was Lennard Koffer.

He'd read about the deadly pests this wide land had to offer.

So, when a mound of hairy mass dropped down upon his head,

He took off through that scrub so fast, he turned the black soil red.

The dropbear, she dropped off half-way; she knew she'd lost her luck.

But f'years to come, *The Flying Dutchman* was his name that stuck.

So, don't believe the rumours, the myths that folk confide;

Dropbears don't drop down on tourists ... unless they need a ride.

The Mystery at Emu Creek

by Jenna Duncan

The campfire crackled in the dying light of the day. Luca poked it gently with a stick.

Molly sat crossed legged on the grass of the Emu Creek campground, twirling her little brother Tommy's hair around her fingers.

Apart from their campsite the grounds of the state park were empty, usual at this time of year. Most tourists preferred the grounds of the more popular rock features in the National Park further west. Normally Molly preferred camping in popular areas, but Luca had insisted on the isolated park and Molly had been outnumbered. Emu Creek it was.

'I'm bored!' cried Tommy, flopping back onto the grass.

As if in response, the door of the tent facing the fire was suddenly thrust open, and Emily emerged with a bowl of marshmallows.

'Who wants to hear a scary story?' Emily whispered trying to sound possessed.

'I do! I do!' cried Tommy jumping up and down.

Emily sat down on the opposite side of the campfire and handed out the marshmallows.

'I've got one,' said Luca, joining Emily on the grass.

'A long time ago at this very campground,' Luca began dramatically, 'a group of schoolgirls and their teacher were on a nature excursion. The sky was overcast, just like today, and the wind was wild whooshing through the trees, howling like a ghost.'

'Oooohhh!' Emily suddenly cried, waving her hands in the air.

'Stop that!' cried Molly.

'May I continue?' Luca asked playfully. 'The group walked along the trail till they came to the small stream.' Luca pointed to the other side of the campground continuing. 'That one we swam in today. There they spread out their picnic lunch.

'After a while, four girls started to get bored and wandered off along the trail. When they didn't return, the teacher decided that they should all go have a look back along the trail for them before returning to the bus.

'They searched for ages but found no sign of the missing girls. The sky darkened further, and the wind picked up so much that the schoolgirls could barely walk in a straight line.

'The teacher decided that they should return to the bus immediately.'

'Without them?' Tommy interrupted.

'Let me finish!' Luca grinned mischievously.

'When the bus came into view,' Luca went on, 'one of the schoolgirls screamed and pointed to the left side of the bus.

'There by the bus rocking eerily from side to side was one of the missing girls.' Luca paused for dramatic effect.

'Dazed and confused, the girl was muttering to herself the same thing over and over again.' Luca suddenly went silent and looked intently at Tommy before whispering 'gone... gone... gone...'

A dingo howled in the distance and an owl hooted from the tree above.

Molly and Tommy screamed in fright.

Luca and Emily burst out laughing.

'Who wants to go explore the trail where the four girls disappeared?!' Emily whispered scarily.

'I do!' cried Luca standing up, 'and since I'm the oldest

and the bravest I lead!'

'And since I'm the second oldest and second bravest, I'll go too!' Emily said keen not to be left behind.

'And I'll stay here with lil' Tommy '' whispered Molly cuddling up close to Tommy.

'Okay your loss,' Emily cried, running to catch up with Luca.

Molly and Tommy watched the two daredevils go as the darkness swallowed them up.

'That was really scary,' whispered Tommy laying his head in Molly's lap.

'It was just a story, little Brother... just a story,' Molly said. 'Hush now.'

She continued to twirl his hair through her fingers, watching the dying fire. 'They won't be long now,' she said, yawning...

* * *

The quiet night was disturbed by a rustling in the bushes some distance from where the campfire dwindled.

Drawn from slumber, Molly looked across to where Luca and Emily had last been seen. The rustling came again, closer this time... and then closer again...

Molly tensed.

Tommy stirred in response, then woke and sat up.

'What is it Molly?' he whispered.

But Molly didn't answer. Instead, she just kept her eyes glued to the bushes just visible on the edge of the campfire's dying light.

The shape of a person shambled out of the bushes muttering to itself.

'Luca, Emily? Is that you?' Molly called out in fright.

The night was silent in reply.

'Luca! Say something! You're scaring me!' Molly called and hugged Tommy closer to her.

Luca stopped just inside the dull ring of campfire light, swaying slightly from side to side. His eyes were distant and dazed. He was muttering distractedly to himself, unaware of Molly and Tommy in front of him.

'Luca?' Molly whispered frightened. 'Where's Emily?'

Luca continued to sway and mutter, 'gone...'

'gone...'

'gone...'

A dingo howled in the distance.

The Power of Faith

by Belinda Meredith

'All you need is a little faith.' Granny Doris always used to say. I loved my Granny, sadly she passed away some time ago; five years, seven months and thirteen days ago to be exact.

I was only six when we moved from the city out to her property 'Holbrook Station' – five hundred acres of land out near Barcaldine. Holbrook Station had been owned by four generations of Holbrook's and it was my Granny's dying wish that her only son, my Dad, would take over the property. I remember the day that we arrived at the farm...

A long, dirt driveway snaked its way through a maze of giant gum trees, stretching from the mailbox all the way to the homestead, over two kilometres away. The homestead was old (built by my Great, Great, Grandfather over one hundred years ago) but cosy. It even came complete with a fireplace, a wrap-around porch and a porch swing. From the swing you could see the grassy green paddocks at the rear of the house; on one side, gently sloping down towards a creek, with bluey-green waters, the other side, gently sloping upwards towards the largest and most magnificent gum tree I had ever laid eyes on.

A couple of months after we moved in, I was given a horse, called Apples and Dad and I built a treehouse in the giant gumtree. I loved to sit in my treehouse and look over the patch work quilt of beautiful colours from the paddocks, trees, and creek below. I had my very own 'Home Among the Gum Trees.' Life on the property was good.

*

That was then. Now the land is barren and dry. It hasn't rained at the property, not one single drop, in five years, seven months and thirteen days. It hasn't rained since Granny Doris passed away. The lovely leaves of the gums are dead and brittle, the green grass, once scattered through the paddocks is gone and the creek is dry. Not a drop of water remains. Varying shades of brown is the only colour to be seen. My Dad was worried, I could tell from the creases and lines that were being etched almost daily onto his forehead and I heard my Mama weeping at night. There was no grass left for the horses or for the sheep to eat, and very little money left to buy stock for them either. I had never seen Mum and Dad so upset. I was upset too. The country was in drought, the worst in our lifetime.

There was no doubt about it; The land was dying, and it needed rain, desperately. But none was coming. I knew this because the Prime Minister said so on the TV last week. The news from the weatherman was not good either. No rain tomorrow, or the next day, or next week, or the week after that. There would be no rain for the foreseeable future. From all reports, it seemed as though the drought would continue. Continue to destroy the land, the home, that I loved so much.

'There's nothing we can do,' Dad said sadly. 'We will have to move back to the city and live with Mum's sister, Aunty Bridget.'

This was the worst news ever! It's not that I didn't like Aunty Bridget, but her house was the size of a shoebox and worse, her yard the size of a postage stamp. What about Apples or my treehouse? Where would they go? What about Granny Doris? This had been her home for her entire life, her memory was everywhere. I couldn't leave her. And I know it would break her heart to think of anyone other than family, living at Holbrook Station. It just didn't feel right.

That night, when I put myself to bed, I was unable to sleep. The pain of Dad's words, forcing fat tears down my face. I cried long and hard, until there were no tears left and I was as dry as the land outside. Unable to sleep, I rose out of bed and stood at my window. The moon was full, and it lit the night sky beautifully. I gazed sadly at the paddocks and my favourite gum tree standing proudly beyond. I stared hard, trying to etch the view firmly in my memory. It was as I stood there that I saw a flicker of movement off in the distance. This was no swaying tree branch; it was more than that. Someone was moving up there!

I rubbed my tired eyes in disbelief; an old woman, was approaching my gum tree. A strong feeling of familiarity came over me. Everything from her slow, graceful walk, to her long, grey hair; Even her clothes, a uniform consisting of a checked shirt, trousers and bright pink gumboots that I had seen countless times before... I would know this person (and particularly those pink gumboots) anywhere. It was Granny Doris!

I strained my eyes harder. It looked as though Granny was beckoning for me, calling me to the tree. Soft as a whisper, like it floated in on the evening breeze, I heard Granny's voice. 'All you need is a little faith.' I rubbed my tired eyes again but this time when I opened them, she was gone.

Granny Doris was on my mind when I awoke the following morning. I wasn't sure if my midnight vision was real or whether it was nothing more than a dream? But I was eager to find out. I dressed quickly and headed through the paddock and towards my tree. I didn't know what I was supposed to do when I got there, but I had faith that there *was* a reason. Standing at the spot where I saw Granny last night, I ran my hand over the bark on the tree's trunk. I was gripped with excitement when I found a burrowed-out hole at the base of the tree. I had visited this tree daily for almost six years and had never come across this before!

I should have been more concerned about snakes or any other animals that might have been living in there; after all, every good bush girl knows that you do not plunge your hand into a hole without checking first. But I was too excited. My hand dove into the cavity in the tree, like it had a mind of its own. With baited-breath and fingers outstretched, desperately searching until... they landed upon a small, hard package!

My hands trembled as I untied the string, holding the brown paper package together. Inside, there was a small, smooth, stone, turquoise in colour and around the size of a golf ball. There was also a note, the paper yellowed, and the edges worn from age. The note said:

This is a magical stone.
It brings blessings and good fortune to whoever possess it.
It has served me well. Now it is time for the stone to have
a new owner.
To unlock its powers, hold the stone tightly and repeat the
following words –
'All you need is a little faith.'

That was all. There was no name or signature. But I knew in my heart that these were the words of Granny Doris. It was after all, her favourite saying. I clutched the stone tightly and repeated the words on the note fifty times, just to be sure.

I wasn't certain what I was supposed to do next, so I waited. I sat under the shade of my gum tree, watching the clouds drift across the blue summers sky. I was lost in thought when something bizarre happened. The sun disappeared. It disappeared as quickly as someone flicking off a light switch. The bright sky of only moments ago, now replaced entirely by dark, black, clouds. Seconds later, the heavens opened and massive, ground drenching drops of rain fell from the sky. It rained solidly for the next fifty days. One day for every time that I recited the spell.

On the fifty first day, the sun came out, shining more brightly than ever, over the now green grass and glistening through the new leaves in the trees. I was quietly admiring its beauty when Dad joined me.

'Do you know what day it is today?' he said.

'Of course. Today would have been Granny's 75th birthday.'

'It would be nice if she were here with us.'

I squeezed the stone in my pocket. 'She is, Dad.'

The drought was finally over. The water tanks were full, there was grass for the animals to eat and vibrant colour from the paddocks and trees surrounded the homestead once more. We no longer needed to move, I didn't have to give up my treehouse and Apples got to stay on the farm.

I had my family; I had the property, but most of all I had faith. I had everything that I would ever need.

The Tree Whisperer

by Sarah Tegerdine

G oing to Grandma and Grandads is always such a treat for Evie and I.

The School holidays provide the perfect excuse to escape the city life for the quiet of the bush. Heading out to the property is always filled with much anticipation for lots of warm hugs, laughter, baking, helping with the farm animals and Grandmas stories!

'We're here!' shouted Mum from the driver's seat.

'Hoorah,' we cheer and scramble to unbuckle our seatbelts.

Grandma and Grandad came out and greet us.

'Ha ha! Come here you little ragamuffins, gives us some hugs,' Grandma shouts!

We race up to them both, 'Right, it's 6'o'clock, dinner

is on the hob, let's have some grub' says Grandad 'Then we can get settled in for the night eh?'

Grandmas stews are always so delicious. I try to eat slowly; I mop up my plate with some fresh crusty bread. After a chat and some dessert, we head up for a bath and bedtime.

Evie and I stalk upstairs with Grandma and my curiosity rises when I see Grandma's hand carved walking staff come out.

'Grandma?' I say, 'We aren't going outside are we?'

'No star gazing walks tonight Lizzy, but I do have a special story to share and my grand old friend here... Well, he will keep us on track,' Grandma chuckles and I look at her inquisitively while Evie rummages around looking for her teddy.

'Ok Girls, are we ready? Snuggle in. Tonight, I'm going to tell you a tale about a young girl called Tilda, she loved exploring and adventure. She always looked for the opportunity to walk anywhere and everywhere. Well almost. Tilda wasn't allowed past a certain boundary on her parent's land. It had always mystified her as to why? She had heard strange stories that sometimes whispers could be heard among in the trees and that the forest could be haunted. However, the indigenous people held the area with such special regard, so she asked herself, how harmful could it really be?'

'One summers day, the winds were high, and she decided to take a run with her dog Shep. He bounded endlessly ahead of her. She struggled to keep up until he stopped. His ears pricked and he took chase towards the boundary line. Tilda called him back to stop and to return but the command was lost on the breeze. For a few moments she stood rooted to the spot. Should she follow? As if in answer she heard Shep barking in the distance and she ran after him.

Tilda approached a foreboding tree line, yet up close it truly was beautiful.

She felt a pull luring her in, she had lost sight of Shep and could no longer hear him barking, so onwards she went.'

'As she walked through the Gum Trees, she felt the warmth of the sun dappling on her skin. Tilda also noticed how calming it was meandering among the trees, then all of a sudden it grew very quiet, she started to feel unusually disorientated. She called out to Shep and heard nothing in response. She felt as though eyes were on her, but she couldn't see anyone. Looking around she kept taking careful steps. Slowly she began to smell smoke in the air, she couldn't see where it was coming from. Fear crept over her knowing quite well she could be in real danger. It was fire season after all. Tilda decided to head back the same way she came in'.

'She hoped Shep had just trotted out and headed home, she had no choice but to decide to leave. When Tilda turned around, she became even more bewildered, she had wondered in quite a distance and everything looked the same. For the first time in her wonderings Tilda realised she was lost. She panicked and started to pick up pace, the smoke was making her cough. Tilda was scared, she felt herself become dizzy and began to think she could hear voices whispering, beckoning her to walk this way and that, her head was swimming, then all went blank'.

Grandma paused, Lizzy gasped, and Evie was fast asleep snuggled in next to her.

'Grandma, you can't stop there, what happened' Lizzy pressed

'Oh Darling, I hadn't stopped, I just took a breather' she smiled, rose an eyebrow with dramatic effect and continued...

'When Tilda woke, she was taken by complete surprise.

She was not in the Gum Tree forest anymore, she found herself on the side of a riverbank. It was encircled by beautiful River Red Gum Trees.'

'Out of nowhere, Shep leaped up on her, his tongue hanging out and enthusiastically started licking her face. It was at this moment she thought she could see movement in the trees. She calmed Shep down and called out, if anyone was there? No one replied, but something strange did happen. The leaves of a beautiful Gum tree began to ripple all at once'.

'Tilda thought she was seeing things, none of the other trees were moving like this. Shep barked happily at Tilda bringing her back to the here and now. It was then she realised a rather beautiful and sturdy branch lying next to her. She pondered, looking back into the trees again, the rustling was still there but less so'.

'She wondered if this branch was left for her? She got up and it helped steady her. Shep was bouncing around. Tilda was quite overwhelmed, still wondering how she got to the riverbank. In her confusion she must have walked here somehow... or did she?'

'That feeling of eyes on her returned, but it was kind and gentle. She called out again to thank whoever or whatever helped her to safety. Even more trees rustled, it was peculiar as the wind had really died down. How were they moving like that? Shep barked again, thankfully she had good hold of the branch. Tilda carefully set off home with Shep, which fortunately wasn't very far away'.

'Her parents embraced her eagerly as they were extremely worried. Bush fires were indeed in the region and they could now evacuate the farm. Tilda swore to herself she would go back, there were mysteries to uncover here'.

'She kept the branch; the wood was beautiful, and her Father carved her a walking staff'.

'A bit like this one I would imagine...' said Grandma, and she chuckled her cheeky chuckle again.

Grandma tucked us both in and kissed us goodnight. I went to sleep feeling quite astonished, but also exhausted.

The next morning, we woke to Grandad cooking pancakes.

'Where is Grandma, Grandad?' I said

'Ah, Good Morning chook she is just out for her morning commune with the Trees' he laughed then corrected himself. 'Ahem, I mean, her morning walk Lizzy, just down by the boundary line.'

I stood gobsmacked, I grabbed my shoes and ran out to find her.

Grandma turned around and greeted me with her wonderful smile, she chuckled and with her she held her beautifully carved staff. 'Grandma' I say, 'Can I come too?'

I had a funny feeling that these school holidays were going to be like no other.

Waratah Wyn

by Amira Beadsmoore

Waratah Wyn of Wentworth Falls was queen of magic brews,
Nattai, Mellong, Woy Woy and more, would come to join her queues.
For years she'd served her clients, with adventure put on hold,
And planned for wild retirement once her business had been sold.

Impatient, as her hair grew grey and bones began to ache,
She shut up shop and settled on a temporary break.
'I'm off to try out something new,' she told the gathered crowds,
'I've left some extra tinctures down at Nelly C. McCloud's.'

Waratah Wyn of Wentworth Falls then left her home address,
She'd packed a bag with everything she'd need, well, more or less.
With ropes and hooks and helmet too, she rocked up at the gorge,
Her guide was dressed in wetsuit with a name tag 'Gulper George'.

'No need for nerves,' she told him, her eyes were all a twinkle,
'I've got this licked, I'm ready, I've even had a tinkle.'

So, Gulper tightened all the belts, he double checked the knots,
He had his work cut out that day because of Wyn's culottes.
They walked together through the gorge as trees gave way to sky,
'Righto, we're 'ere' young Gulper said, 'You sure you wanna try?'
Waratah Wyn of Wentworth Falls said, 'Never, in my days!
Not TRY, but DO, that's how I live, lead on, show me the way.'

Young Gulper George clipped to the rocks and stood upon the ledge,
He turned around, pointed his toes and pushed off from the edge.
Now it was time for Wyn to go, she clipped onto the rocks,
But, as she pushed, a sedge got caught inside her orange crocs.
It pulled her right off balance and she flipped around and round.
When, finally, she came to rest her head was pointing down.
Waratah Wyn of Wentworth Falls could see her guide below,
She knew her blue could give him cause to scoff at her and crow.

Not one to whinge or take defeat, she looked to help herself,

And then she saw the answer on a craggy granite shelf.

A glint of golden stems told her this plant was just the one,

To give her all the grease required to make the jammed ropes run.

She swayed and swung whilst wrapped up tight in twisted ropes and cloth,

Much like a caterpillar feels till it becomes a moth.

She swung and swung, the rope it creaked, young Gulper closed his eyes.

The waterfall crashed down, as her culottes stuck to her thighs.

She gave each swing her best attempt, not easy in that pose,

Just then a cockatoo flew down and perched upon her nose.

Its feathers caused a twitching and her eyes began to squint,

The cockatoo, he chuckled, then he flew off at a sprint.

A loud explosion from Wyn's nose provided perfect push,

And as her head came up to it, her teeth tore at the bush.

She chewed and chewed the stems and leaves to make a magic ooze,

That dripped down to the twisted ropes and made them run real smooth.

Old Wyn descended on the rope to meet George down below,

While on a rock a dragon basked just taking in the show.

Young Gulper led the way back top, he didn't say a word,

He knew, deadset, that anything was bound to sound absurd.

Waratah Wyn of Wentworth Falls was glad she'd done the drop,
but now, she knew, she'd rather be back in her old tin shop.

Waratah Wyn of Wentworth Falls still mixes magic brews,
but secretly she harbours thoughts involving sea canoes.

Wombats Save the Day

by Jeanie Axton

Mrs Wombat first heard the roar
As Mr Wombat cried out at the door.
'Wildlife please all come inside,
'Our borrows the perfect place to hide.'

In came the lizards one by one.
Skinks followed next with their young.
A family of bush mice scuttled past,
Four little legs running fast.

A wallaby hopped from behind a tree
Asking to enter, he wiggled and squeezed.
A snake slithered past giving all a fright
However, he calmed each with, 'I will not bite.'

King parrots flew in as the fire drew near.
The wombats shuffled them to the rear.
An owl hooted as she looked for a bed,
A soft cosy place to lay her head.

Finally, an echidna came to the door
Wanting to know, 'Could you fit one more?'
He pronounced he may be a little bit prickly
As the smoke outside had made him sickly.

The flames burnt through the bush outside.
Without these burrows all could have died.
Hooray! To the wombats for finding a way
To shelter our wildlife and save the day.

Printed in Australia
AUHW010002261020
336121AU00012B/47